OUR WAR

BY RICHARD MAVERICK

[signature]

9-12-21

THOUGHTS FROM THE AUTHOR

After September 11, 2001, I believed a war in this country was an extreme possibility. I thought it would most likely be the result of a mass coordinated terrorist attack, unlike anything we had seen yet. I immediately packed what would be the first of my "go bags" and began talking to others to see if I was the only one out there who felt the way that I did.

As the years passed, I still try my best to remain prepared in the event of such a tragic event. As my understanding of what a "go bag" should consist of based on my individual needs, my bag changed.

My belief in war has not changed; what has changed, however, is what I believe will be the ultimate cause for such horror in my lifetime. It has become more apparent to me now that the war this country is facing will not be caused by Islamic extremism, we will most likely cause it, we the people, and our hatred for each other will be what destroys this great nation.

There is a massive political divide, being pushed by those who wish to have absolute power over We The People. In 2008 I was told by old rich white people that if I did not vote for their candidate for president, then I was a racist. During his first four years in office, the "other side" stood by and played the "it wasn't me" game, blaming everything that could go wrong on failed policies instead of trying anything to fix them. Then I was told if I did not vote for him again, I was still racist. Still, the "other side" played the "it wasn't me" game, and yet they did nothing but complain about what was being done with no resolution to fix it.

In 2016 I was informed by the same old rich white people from before that if I did not vote for the old rich white woman, not only was I racist, but I was also Islamophobic, homophobic, sexist, and deplorable. I do believe strongly in the power of suggestion; you tell someone something long enough; they and those around them may very well start to believe it. How many from the side of name-calling are under the belief at this very moment? How many people who never had a racist bone in their bodies now believe they are racist? How many people are now fighting an enemy they didn't know they had until they heard the rhetoric they have been force-fed because people are not getting their absolute power? Politics at this time have become a form of hate, in my opinion, a reason to be violent and disrespectful to our fellow countrymen and women.

We live in a nation now where so-called adults scream at children for wearing hats that support the current sitting United States president. Politicians call for the harassment of anyone who supports the president, including his staff. Celebrities that depict the death of our president and some who tell us, "maybe this country needs another civil war."

I wonder if those so-called celebrities and politicians believe the men and women they pay to protect them will still be protecting them while we ordinary folk fight a war? Do they think that they are so important those people will let their families die to keep them safe from harm? I can assure you that those men and women do not get paid enough to sit by and let their families die. Meanwhile, the other side sits and continues to play the "it wasn't me" game, doing nothing at all to help the president, we the people voted into office, not a perfect man, but the right man for the job.

I think what we need now is to VOTE away all our career politicians, start fresh, red, or blue it does not matter. If they have been in office longer than one or two terms, vote them gone. Take away their power and their platform that they are using to divide this great nation. Vote against your "party" if that's what it takes to get some fresh faces, new ideas, and real change for We the People.

I wonder if the career politicians would still have such a powerful voice to call you racist if they lost their jobs. Would they still call for the harassment of others? Would people still be ok with it if they did? If they did, then you can guess what their goal was all along. I recall learning in high school about a man in 1930's Germany who pushed the same kind of division against his people, while others in Germany stood by and let him do it.

What else could we as a country do to combat this hate epidemic? How about having a conversation with someone you would not usually talk to? If you hear your neighbor shooting in his back yard, why not ask them why they own a gun? If your neighbor is a single mother with no job, why not ask her why she doesn't work? Take the time to try and understand their point of view; do not push yours, listen to theirs. Have a civil conversation about your differences; if you simply can't do that, then talk about something else, anything else. Talk about sports, the weather, your families, anything else that will keep you from dividing yourselves more. Find a reason to be friends with someone you know on a political level you know you will disagree with. If we can do that, we will beat the agenda set forth by our elected leaders. We can overcome hate and intolerance.

Make no mistake about it. We are on a scale that I do believe is tipping closer and closer to a war that NO ONE wants. I am not afraid to fight; I am, however, fearful of my children growing up in a war-torn nation. War in this country will be the end of us; once it starts, there will be no end. There are no less than a half dozen other countries that would love to see this great nation at war with itself, fighting with each other while they slip in the back door with ill intent. For the sake of our children, we must come back together before we destroy their future and the future of this great nation.

The story you are about to read is a work of fiction. Names, characters, businesses, places, events, and incidents are either the product of my imagination or used in a fictitious manner. Any resemblance to actual persons living or dead, or actual events is purely coincidental.

How far from reality this story remains will be left entirely up to WE THE PEOPLE!!!!

Dedicated to my children,
may you never know the reality of my nightmares.

CHAPTER 1

July 4, when the so-called activists decided to start their protests, as they called them, claiming that the celebrated holiday was somehow racist. Riots erupted in several major cities. Buildings burned, attacks were made on law enforcement, and some small explosions occurred throughout the day. Unfortunately, however, things didn't end when the sunset. Chaos continued throughout the week, keeping everyone on edge.

It was the following Saturday, the day of our Cattlemen's Ball; Dad asked me to run to our warehouse in Goldbeach to pick up a bunch of products that we had packed that week for shipping. I hopped into my car, making the thirty-minute drive. I had just turned onto Central Avenue when three blocks ahead of me, town hall exploded. I quickly pulled off on a side street and kept on my path to our warehouse; only now, I was hauling ass. I pulled into the parking lot fast and jumped out of the car without even turning off the engine. I popped the trunk; as quickly as I exited, I grabbed the go-bag and weapons bag, making my way inside as quickly as possible, locking the door behind me.

Inside my primary weapons bag was my helmet, battle belt, and plate carrier; throwing that gear on quickly, I then started stuffing pouches with shotshell cards and pistol magazines. Grabbing my shotgun, I made my way around the building, setting perimeter alarms on all the windows and doors; it was going to be a long day waiting out the possibilities before nightfall. I got my handheld radio out and started checking to see who from my team was around.

"This is Six-Eight Awfully hot for this time of year. I say again this is Six-Eight Awfully hot for this time of year, over."

Nothing but static came back at me. Either the team was out of range, or they were already at the primary location.

I looked down at my watch; it was only 4:00 pm. Four lousy hours had gone by. I had heard gunfire and several smaller explosions in the time I'd been hunkered down. Pacing back and forth between the hallways, avoiding the windows, trying my best to stay calm and quiet so I could hear if any glass was breaking, it occurred to me I needed something to relax my mind. I dug into my go bag and pulled out a small travel humidor, cracked it open, and pulled out a cigar. I sat against a wall, cut my cigar, then lit it. How soothing that sweet smell was at that moment. My heart rate began to slow, and my mind stopped racing. Finally, something more than chaos, finally some transparent thought process.

I went into one of our old shipping rooms, where we still had some tables set up and dug out my maps. I started marking where I thought roughly the bulk of the gunfire and explosions came from. My best bet seemed to be making my way down Route 5. Unfortunately, that would also put me in the god damn open for much longer than I really cared to be. Making my way into the bathroom to top off my canteens, I noticed a Hispanic male, from the window, looking around the outside, and then he waved over his buddies. I pulled my shotgun into my shoulder, keeping it ready, heart rate starting to increase. At the distance I was from him, the red dot on my gun covered most of his face. Just then, he said, "Ok, guys, we're clear." and off they went in my car.

I dropped back, breathing heavy and shaking a little thankful I didn't have to pull the trigger as it would have brought more than just him and his couple friends down on me. Then I would have been royally screwed. I realized that if they decided to check things out more, they were sure to come before darkness finally settled; *it's time to get out of here,* I told myself. I topped off my canteens, did a fast gear check making sure all ammo pouches were full, and medkit secured on my belt and gave a quick final lube to both my primary and secondary weapons.

Checking the windows on the Route 5 side of the building, I noticed most people had drawn their curtains so that no one could see in, hoping to be left alone. I cracked the door ever so lightly, trying to see what might be in my way right off the bat, hugging the wall watching both in front of me, and continually checking my six to be sure that no one was behind me. I managed to make my way down to a building I always thought was a firehouse. It turns out it was just another one of those social clubs where you had to be a member to drink. The place was closed. I picked the lock, got in, and shut the door quickly behind me. I was honestly no more than one hundred yards from the warehouse, but maybe no one would bother me there, at least for an hour or two. Then perhaps I could get a better plan.

Knowing Route 5 was going to suck, it was still my best possible route to get the hell out of town, but darkness must be on my side for this to work. With all the explosions, some small arms fire, and sirens still in the not too far distance, I decided to get out my "squirrel pistol." It's a 22-long rifle caliber pistol with a mini red dot sight I had at that time used for backpacking and camping to shoot small animals to cook while out. Making sure the optic was on, I shot out streetlights one at a time in between other loud noises hoping that no one would notice the sound of such a small-caliber pistol. Distance not so much in my favor with this gun. I was able to shoot out three on each side of the street. *Let's hope darkness falls soon so I can get closer to home.*

Cars had been flying by for hours. Trying to get out of the city, and the sun was finally going down. Time check said it was quarter after nine, time to move my ass. Cracking the front door, checking as far as I can see with minimal exposure. I was trying to see if there was anyone on Route 5 that was going to be an immediate threat. Looked clear enough to make it to the next building for cover. Cars were still passing trying to get out. I had to be careful that they didn't light me up and give away where I was at to people that were on the streets. Moving from one building to the next for cover, I was finally on the corner of central avenue. Two streetlights up, EMS and first responders were still working on getting out the wounded and dead, law enforcement was busy securing the scene trying to keep the already very pissed off local personnel out of the way. The gunfire was still the sound of the night but didn't seem to be in the immediate blast zone. Even where I was hunkered down, I could smell burnt flesh and smoke as it filled the air.

It was time to keep my fat ass moving, one building to the next, slowly, staying out of sight as best as I could. The sound of gunfire was fainter; however, I knew there would be more the closer I got to the next town. I ran up behind the Moose Club, watching for any sign of trouble. Cars were still speeding by trying to get away from the city, but no one seemed to notice me kneeled tight on the corner of the building. I finally dashed across the street to the tree line. Working my way around an abandoned hotel then past the old folk's home, I was finally better concealed and ready for a break. I got far enough into the woods that you probably couldn't have seen me, but I could still see the road as it was going to be my guide home. About a hundred yards away was a house, so I moved up along the side, one hundred yards past it before cutting across the back of it, one hundred yards across the back then back down the opposite side. It seems like a lot of unneeded movement; however, it makes sense if you're trying to avoid conflict with people that are merely scared and will probably shoot at anything that moves.

I kept on moving, and every time I saw a house in the distance, I'd take preventive measures to avoid detection just like before. I was moving at a steady pace, not running by any means but more of a brisk careful walk, making sure as to where my feet were landing so I wouldn't trip and get hurt or worse, letting someone know where I was. The moon, though only half was showing, was very bright, and the sky was clear, giving just enough light to navigate successfully with minimal noise. It had now been several hours since the initial explosion that rocked the city, and I was still very much on the move, headed home. I finally came to an abandoned house on Route 5 that was a predetermined checkpoint and resting spot I had selected. Keeping my distance from the house, however, due to the fact it sat right off the road and I really didn't want to be in there when someone else stopped because they had the same idea. I sat against a tree and started relaxing a bit, got out my canteen, and mixed in a Gatorade packet to add some flavor to what turned out to be piss warm water. I was only a few short miles from the city, but in prior planning, I had figured if I wound up on foot in an emergency, it would take three days to get the thirty miles home safely.

All of a sudden, I heard what sounded like a group of guys yelling at another group of people. I got out my binoculars, though hard to see a lot, and could see a group of what looked like gang members, with red X's on their shirts, shoving three women and four men into the abandoned house. Understand something I'm no god damn hero. When I put plans on the drawing board for this type of emergency, I wasn't going to go all over town to find a fight, my goal was to get home, and no one would get in my way of that. In this case, however, the very fact that it was this close to me, and those people seemed to be in severe trouble, I made the decision to act.

Getting close to the house, I could see that there were four gang members with small arms. They stationed one guy outside to keep watch until it was his turn to get in on the action they had planned. I dropped my bug out bag on the ground, quietly taking my field knife off the pack. I snuck up behind the guy outside, putting my hand over his mouth and shoving my field knife through the side of his neck, ripping it forward, damn near decapitating him, gently setting his body onto the ground, hoping no one inside noticed. I peeked into the window to see that they had tied one of the women up and stripped her clothes from her, one of the men was thrashing to get to her, two of the remaining skinnies started beating him severely.

"I'm going to fuck your wife," said one skinny to the beaten man. "Then, my friends will take turns with her." He turned to one of the other men and said, "Your wife will be next, and then your mother."

I went around to the back door of the house and snuck in, making my way slowly to the room that they had the people held against their will. Bringing my shotgun up into my chest, I burst into the room, firing at the two guys who were keeping the men and other women away from the woman about to be raped. The third guy had just gotten down onto the floor on top of her. He sat up and back quickly "please have mercy; we only wanted to have some fun with them" I didn't say a word to that piece of shit, and I didn't hesitate to pull the trigger to the rear putting buckshot into his face.

I held my hand out to the woman and said, "We need to move from this location and right fucking now." She took my hand, and I helped her up. I ran over and checked on her husband. He was in bad shape. They had hit him in the face with the buttstock of their rifles and hammered on his ribs bad.

"Can you move?" I asked him. He grunted as he shook his head, indicating he could. One of the other men there was his son. "I'll help my dad move." said the young man.

I looked at the woman's brother and told him to gather whatever weapons and ammunition he could carry. We got outside through the back door. I grabbed my bug out bag throwing it on.

"Follow me, try to keep pace with me, and in line with me as well, you'll be least likely to fall and get hurt that way," I said to them.

The woman who had been stripped of her clothes asked, "Are there extra cloths in that bag of yours? All of mine were ripped, and I can't keep running through the woods naked".

"Once we get to the backup checkpoint, I'll get you the extra clothes from my bag, but right now, we need to keep moving away from this location as I'm sure someone heard the gunfire," I responded to her.

It took about thirty minutes to get to my pre-selected backup checkpoint: another abandoned house and the last one on this route home.

"Stay here while I check the place out," I told them.

I went in, making sure no one else was inside the house before motioning them to come in. I wouldn't have used the house as a rest stop. However, having seven extra people, one of whom needed clothing and one who needed some medical attention and needed rest. I decided that going into the house may be in the group's best interest.

Once inside, I dropped to my knees, throwing my bag on the floor, getting out a tee shirt and a pair of boxers, I handed them to the naked woman, "Here this is all I have," I said while trying hard not to look her in the face.

"Thank you," she replied.

I got a disposable ice pack from inside my med kit, "Put this on your ribs for a few minutes then on your face," I told her husband.

I told them all they should rest as we would only be at that location for two to three hours max since the sun would be up in four hours. About an hour in, the woman who had been sexually assaulted walked into the room I was in.

"Who are you?" she asked, bearing in mind it was dark out, and it's not like the abandoned house I rescued them from had electric hooked up.

"It's not important who I am. What is important is that you and your family are now safe," I responded.

Just then, from the doorway, her son said, "That's a normal response from you, William."

The woman was in shock, you see she wasn't just any woman, her name was Ann, and she was my ex-wife. She had left her husband some years back to be with me, and not long after she and I had gotten married, she left me for her ex-husband. During that time, her son and I had gotten remarkably close, even after that time, I still felt like he was my own child.

"How did you know it was me?" I asked him

"I saw your Losers tattoo in the moonlight when we were walking here, I remember seeing you outside the tattoo studio the day you got it," he said

"Robert, you need to get some rest," I told him. He smiled and walked out of the room.

Ann was in complete shock. I looked at her. "Where the fuck were you going?"

"We were headed to your house; I knew no matter what you would keep us all safe," she said.

Just then, her brother Robbie came into the room with an overly aggressive tone and attitude "We need to get back to the cars our guns are in the trunk, and we need them."

"Fuck you, Robbie, you want those guns, then go back on your own and get them because I'm headed home," I replied, "Now get some fucking sleep we leave at first light."

Dawn came, I got everyone up and ready to move. I asked Ann's husband if he would be able to make it on foot without help. He assured me he would be able to keep up. We left the house and went back into the woods, deeper like I had been moving before. After about four hours of making movement as quickly and quietly as possible, we took a break. Ann's dad was having a bit of trouble catching his breath, which concerned me as he had a heart condition. We rested much longer than I had planned, but I didn't want her dad to drop dead from a heart attack en route. I decided to slow our pace, hike for two hours then rest for thirty minutes might be a much better idea. At this point, Ann had more questions as I expected she would.

"Where were you coming from?" she asked

"I was at the warehouse getting stuff to ship out on Monday," I replied

"When were you there," she stated

"I got there at noon if I recall, around five my car was stolen, and I decided to start the movement home sooner than expected due to being on foot in a city falling apart on itself," I explained

"If you had messaged me and told me you were there, we could have stopped and picked you up, we drove right past there," she said with heartache in her eyes.

"First off, we haven't spoken in months, and even if I did message you, you probably wouldn't have read it, let alone the fact if you did read it, stop and pick me up, I would have been just as screwed as you all were when I found you," with a growl in my voice.

"William I'm so sorry for what I put you through," she started to say

"Keep that shit to yourself because no one here wants to hear it. My only mission right now is to make it home. I can make it there easier if I leave your asses here." I interrupted

"You wouldn't really leave us here, would you?" she asked

"keep bringing up old useless shit, and I will," I told her, "for your sake, let's not do this again sometime."

You could see the hurt in her eyes just as I turned and walked away from her. I took out what food I had in my bag. I split it between Robert and Ann's parents. After thirty minutes, I told the group to get on their feet as it was time to keep moving. We started moving forward again, after what seemed to be two of the most prolonged hours of my life, we stopped again. I swear if we moved any slower, we would move backward in time. I knew I couldn't safely rush them, though. We took another break. Robbie was still complaining to his wife and mother about being "forced" to leave their guns in the truck.

"Robbie you have two AKs and a hi-point carbine between you and your wife, so pick one, then you can play Rambo to impress her," I barked at him

"It's not about playing Rambo as you put it, it's about keeping my family safe," he shouted

"Really? You were doing a bang-up job keeping them safe on your knees, crying like a bitch when I found you all in that house. I'm your absolute best chance at staying alive, keep your bullshit to yourself or walk your fat ass back to your truck I don't need your dead weight keeping me from where I need to be," I said

He turned and walked away, instantly his mom looked like she wanted to talk to me, but I gave her the "I don't fucking care about your opinion" look, and she walked away as well.

I told them all again; it was time to keep moving. After yet another two hours, we took another break. I did yet another radio check at this time, still no reply from Two-Five. After another short break, we got back on the move. This cycle kept up until we reached Amish territory north of my home.

We hunkered down in a barn belonging to an Amish man named Levi. He worked for us doing odd jobs from time to time. We had been there all of ten minutes when he walked in with some food.

"You all must be hungry," he said

"I haven't eaten in almost three days at this point, thank you very kindly, Levi," I responded

Levi began passing out what food he had with him to the others first then to me. He left only moments later; I'm guessing he wanted to let us eat in private.

I pulled out my radio. "Two-Five this is Six-Eight, Two-Five this is Six-Eight it's awfully hot for this time of year" there was silence for a couple of seconds and then

"But not as sticky as two summers ago Six-Eight it's damn good to hear your voice, over."

"Two-Five we are currently five miles north from your location, how copy," I said,

"Good copy, Six-Eight see you in the morning," the voice on the radio responded.

Get rest; we will move again at dawn, I told the group. I knew we could probably make it home with the moonlight if we used the roads, but I didn't want to chance a car spotting us, no idea who would be friendly or not at this moment, and still no idea just yet what entirely happened. I once again pulled a cigar from my bag to help relax my mind a bit. The smoke filled the air with hints of leather and spice. I was tired myself, at this point, it had been days since I had slept, but there was just no real way that I could trust anyone in this group aside from Ann and her son to have my back. However, I wasn't going to ask a boy to do my job for me, he still had some innocence, and if I could help it, he was going to keep it as long as possible. Moments later there was a knock at the barn door, it was Levi and one of his sons-in-law

"You looked tired earlier William, this is my son-in-law Chris, he is going to keep watch for you guys while you get some sleep, if there's anything that needs your attention, he will wake you up" stated Levi

"Levi, I can't thank you enough for all you've done for us tonight," I told him as I shook his hand.

Morning came, back into the woods we went, we were five miles from home. I talked with Ann's father for a moment. I figured we could make this trip without stopping, but we would go slow for his benefit. I told him that he would walk up front with me, and I would not move any faster than he could. After about two hours, I could see the trailhead that ran down the back of my property about one hundred yards out.

"Two-Five this is Six-Eight, we are one hundred yards North of your position. Hold your fire; I say again one hundred yards North of your position hold your fire how copy?" I said,

"Good copy, Six-Eight see you soon," replied the voice over the radio.

As I walked down the driveway towards my house, I could see everyone who had been there for the barbeque, they had been here for a couple of days now, and they were scared. It was just at that moment I heard "Daddy, daddy, daddy, daddy" with my little girl running towards me

CHAPTER 2

That's right; I'm a family man. Married with two children. My daughter, who was only three when all this started, my son was five at the time. I grew up in small-town USA, literally a one-stoplight town. I spent most of my life working the family business, which included a lot of traveling and now a family farm where we raised pork and beef for food and profit. I joined the military right out of high school but was discharged for a blown-out knee with only eighteen months in the reserves. I went to work for my father almost as soon as I got home. I spent the next fifteen plus years traveling from city to city doing trade shows. In my late twenties, I decided to start training in hand-to-hand combat about an hour north of my homestead, and after nearly four years, I got my first-degree black belt. During my time training there, I started attending firearm training classes with some of the most dangerous men alive and started in competitive shooting sports. It was through a retail store that my family had opened that I had slowly begun meeting the crazy assholes that would later become "the team."

Two-Five, he was my best friend, primary training partner, and godfather to my daughter. I met him at our shop. He wondered in one day asking me all sorts of gun and gear questions. Honestly, he seemed like the kind of guy that no matter what advice you gave him, he was going to be too full of himself to listen. It turns out I was way off. He started coming in more and more with more and more questions; he even started helping in the shop and later the farm. A competitive shooter who I was finally, after a few years, able to talk into trying some of the combative based firearms class as I had taken. He was a bit younger than me, and honestly, he was a bit of an asshole. Tattooed with a big beard, he worked at a place that made dental molds or something goofy like that. He still lived at home but was responsible, reliable, and probably the best shot in the group.

One-Three, yet another member of the team I met through my time in the shop. He was one of the older team members at nearly fifty years old. A married father of two awesome boys. His wife was a professional marathon runner and extreme fitness buff. He worked as a lawn care technician, as he would explain to us, and played in a couple of different heavy metal bands. Absolutely loyal to those who stood with him, he tended to keep his cool when everyone else around him was losing their minds. He also shot competitive shooting sports and started training with firearms just like I did. He spent two years in the Air Force, discharged honorably. He never dwelled on his time in the military and generally never brought it up. Nothing really could throw him out of focus, well except for a nice pair of tits.

Six-One, he was the youngest on the team. A married father of four including twin boys, he often referred to as "the assholes." He worked at a steel plant when we met, with dreams of becoming a police officer in our local sheriff's office. He was a bit quieter than the rest of us, probably because we never really let him get too much in when we were all talking. I met him through the shop like the others. Got him talked into training and shooting at the matches we all went to, and he was hooked. Personally, I think he hung around as much as he did to gain as much knowledge as he could from us, even though we were all still learning sometimes on the fly. He was a cigar aficionado, much like me, and certainly appreciated an excellent single malt.

Two-Eight was the oldest on the team at over fifty years old. Light brown skin, I always thought he was Italian, so I asked him one day his background, seventy-five percent white, twenty-five percent black. He joked that the "brothers" in the military said he was not black enough to count. He was married with one child, who went off to college the year before the war. He spent twenty years in the military, and the only thing I could tell you is he went to sapper school as a combat engineer. He was smart on a lot of topics; he liked the idea of being on a team, but with an individual task of winning allowed him to focus on the work that needed to be done. He worked relentlessly for as long as it took to accomplish the task at hand. We met at the school where I got my first-degree black belt. He finished his training there years later as a third-degree black belt. After I had to leave the school due to yet another knee injury, he contacted me on social media, looking for some weapons training, and well he pushed to every class with us becoming a member of the team.

Six-Six was the newest member of the team, met him through my friendship with Two-Four. New to the shooting sports and firearms training, however, he desperately wanted to learn and was always asking for advice on gear and gun selection. He was married, no children, thirty-one years of age, avid hunter and mechanic. We started hanging out a lot before things went to hell. We drank some bourbon, and well, as they say, the rest is history. I knew he had our backs as we did his.

Two-four, there's not much to say about him. I knew him for several years. Great guy, but stuck in the "the Marines taught me all I need to know about guns" mentality. He was an Emergency medical technician and volunteer firefighter. He was Puerto Rican, married a woman half his age who was whiter than all of us combined. We used to joke she was obsessed with her parent's gardener when she was little, and that's why she married his ass.

Three-Three was my childhood best friend. A married father of two children. He was the extreme opposite of the rest of us. He was a liberal, didn't own guns, and said he never would, and he'd only handle a gun if I were around to keep him in line. He moved from the small town we both grew up in and started his life in the city. He always said if war ever broke out in the US, that he would be glued to my side. That way, he could learn all he could to help keep his family safe. Typically that attitude pissed me off, but hell, he was my brother, not just my friend. We had known each other for nearly three decades; how could I tell him no?

Doc was a combat medic with three tours in Vietnam with a Ranger company in the Army. At seventy-two years old, he had pretty much done it all. Owned his own business', was a radio DJ, worked on farms, and owned his own farm, recently opened a bunch of rental cabins on the same property I lived on. He was my hero though I never told him, but then what son would tell his father that? When shit started, he became our medic and our doctor. The very same man who once told me I was nuts for setting aside extra supplies for just in case such a need raised, yet he did the very same.

We called ourselves "Losers," a funny name for a group of alpha males; however, it had an excessively significant meaning to us. During a time in human history when it was considered "cool" to play the knockout game against unexpected innocent bystanders, we chose to be losers. When it was "cool" to kidnap a mentally disabled kid and torture him on Facebook Live because of the color of his skin, we chose to be losers. When it became "cool to attack, assault, and kill law enforcement officers, we were ever prouder to be losers. Don't get me wrong; we were not "perfect," and we did not perceive ourselves to be better than anyone. We made our share of mistakes like every other human on the planet. It wasn't about being a perfect person. There's no such thing. It was about being a decent person, a kind person, an overall good human being. A role model for our children and not one of the monsters we told them exist in the world. We made a pact to group together in the event of society breaking down because well, there's strength in numbers. We decided to use numbered call-signs to identify each other, in the event the war ever ended, this would make it hard for anyone to identify everyone in the group by name, in the event we ever faced prosecution for our actions. We didn't wear camouflage uniforms. We were ordinary guys, not soldiers. We believed it was more important to train for the part than we did to look the part. Don't misunderstand me; we had no problem with the guys that showed up to classes wearing Salomon shoes or Arcteryx pants. We did have a problem with the guys that bought that stuff because their favorite Instagram "instructor" wore them. Usually, you'd see us show up to classes in Wrangler jeans or Wrangler outdoor pants and combat boots. Being in the surplus business, the boots were cheap enough for us to afford them to save our money for guns and gear. As I said earlier, we trained together with some of the most dangerous men on this earth. Competed together, and when it was time for a birthday party, they were always invited. They were family, my kids' "uncles." They were more family to me than some of my bloodlines ever was.

Two-Five met me at the main house "Damn glad to see you brother, any trouble getting here besides the obvious?" he laughed

I replied, "It's a long story. I'll brief you on later, tell me what you know."

According to the ham radio, there was a severe uprising from possible far-left groups, wanting dead white people or other people's money. Other voices on the radio suggested a potential rebellion from far-right groups wanting to whiten America or just simply people who wanted to watch the world burn. Honestly, information was still way to unclear to get a fix on what caused it.

Aside from the team and the few that I ended up bringing with me, there were nearly one hundred people at my homestead for the big family barbecue. Including my grandparents, which made me happy to know they were here, instead of stuck about an hour north of my home on a good drive. They were in their eighties at this time, my grandmother was confined to a wheelchair, my grandfather had a hard time getting around himself, and his memory got fuzzy from time to time. He walked up to me with tears in his eyes the second he saw me and hugged me. He had been worried sick if I was ok or not. Both of my sisters were there as well, one older and one younger than myself. One lived in the city one hour north of my home. She tried to live back closer to home for a few years, but as it turned out, the "country life" was no longer for her. She moved back to the city, and my other sister took over the house she lived in, which happened to be where we raised our cows. She had a college education and worked at a hospital on the surgical floor, which naturally in her mind made her smarter than everyone she also had her head, at thirty years of age, stuck firmly up my father's ass. Her twin brother shared her slot as the youngest child. He moved to the city as well, chasing a girl. She taught him that it was ok to be trash, treating people with absolute disrespect because well, if you're not going do everything for them, there is no reason they should care at all about you. I don't hate him, but I have absolutely no respect for him or his so-called family. If they couldn't steal it, get it for free, or screw someone out of it, they didn't want it. He was proof you can't choose your blood, but you sure as hell can choose who you call family.

.

CHAPTER 3

As a team, we planned for such an event as best as we could. We did what we called a group "buy share," things that would be needed for the group would be bought as a team but divided up. For instance, I bought all the toilet paper I possibly could, the others, of course, bought for their homes but nothing more than that. One-three bought all the dental hygiene products he thought that the group would need, again the rest of us bought for our homes but nothing more than that unless we needed something extra or special. Of course, I could go on with a hundred other examples, but I think you got the idea. We all chipped in for case lots of ammo, cold-weather gear, and other things the team could benefit from. We bought radios for communication between team members. We also bought extra radios that we would pass out to people on the surrounding roads near my homestead and the farms. This way, they could let us know if anything was headed our way.

The overall idea behind the plan was to, of course, keep everyone safe, but we also had to try and keep everyone busy so that they would hopefully be able to stay calm. Give everyone a job to do, a reason to remain focused on something, and hopefully build a community within the chaos while letting the team worry about the other stuff. The plan involved getting the names of everyone present at the time of a critical incident. If I was not present at the time, that job fell into the hands of Two-Five. After getting some much-needed hugs from my children, Two-Five handed me a clipboard with the names, ages, genders, and real-world occupations of all those that were still there during the three days I was en route to home.

"Two-Five I'll meet you in the cave in thirty minutes to discuss the plan, Six-One you have command until we return," I said.

I walked into my house with my wife and kids right on my heels. The first thing I did was strip off my plate carrier, helmet, and t-shirt. My wife instantly started complaining as I expected she would.

"Who the fuck is that bitch you brought back with you?" she screamed at me

I was then forced to explain that along the way, I ran into my ex-wife and her family. After getting them out of what would be the end of their lives, I thought it best to bring them home with me. They had already been on their way to the house for protection anyway. She was less than impressed hearing that the woman I brought home was, in fact, my ex-wife, for whom she had never met nor seen a picture of before that day. I then explained to her that we needed all the able-bodies we could get. Still less than impressed, she stormed out of the room.

I finished taking off my three-day-old clothing, hopped in the bathroom, and did a quick field wash up. I Got redressed and headed for the basement of my house. We called the basement "the cave" it was a place that we had predetermined that only team members would ever be allowed to go into. We had set the room up as what one might call a study or man cave. Books on the shelves and maps of all surrounding areas on the wall. Ammo on pallets, fully loaded magazines and side saddles on the shelves, a fully stocked cabinet humidor, and a fully stocked team bar. It was our place for stress relief and to go over plans such as the one at hand.

Two-Five was waiting for me when I got down there. I grabbed a cigar first, lit it hot, and got started figuring out jobs for all. The first thing we did was go over official shooter assignments. The unit was broken into two teams, Alpha and Bravo. Two-Five was the Bravo team leader, and I was the Alpha team leader. We would run on two separate twelve-hour shifts. Our team members would run eight-hour shifts. I assigned One-Three and Six-Six to Bravo, keeping Two-Eight and Six-One for Alpha. Shooters would pick an aid; this person would be responsible for making sure the team member got food while on their shift and had plenty of water. Aids would run the same shift as their assigned shooter. My aid would be Three-Three, though part of the team, he had zero training at all, and his only weapons experience was when we used to shoot bb guns as children.

Next on our list was all who were present and giving them jobs, all though shit had literally hit the fan throughout the entire country, we needed to keep order and keep going. The only logical way to do this was to figure out what the group would need and assign jobs to people. The tasks would help them to keep their minds off what was happening around them and give them a sense of purpose. Such jobs needed to be filled included gardeners to take care of the vegetables, fruits, and herbs that we had been growing. Gatherers, people who would wander the property looking for wild-growing vegetables, fruits, and herbs. Wood gatherers, people that would gather firewood for all the cabins, pavilion, main headquarters, and shooting positions. Hunters, they would only shoot enough for the group to eat for the day, they used makeshift suppressors to hide the sound of gunfire from those around us. If they had a bad day hunting, we planned to butcher a pig. Childcare, these people needed to attend to the children by making sure they move as a group to the places they needed to be. A radio person, their job would consist of listening to the short-wave radio listening for any clues as to what happened and or possible bad guy movements. Teachers, fitness instructors, cooks, food preparation personnel, medics, and water gatherers. I could go on, but again you got the idea.

"Get everyone to the pavilion in one hour so we can go over assignments," I said to Two-Five.

"Roger," he replied.

I pushed on the talk button on my radio. "Six-One, do you copy."

"Copy boss," he replied.

"Take One-Three and start handing out radios to the farms around us, make sure they are good, tell them when they are ready, we can begin trading goods," I told him as I started up the stairs to head out.

"Wilco." He said

As we walked out back, you could hear people whispering, scared of what was going on, fear because we didn't have reliable answers. I walked to the front of the group, where my father was standing, trying to calm everyone down as they continually asked what was going on and what the plan was.

"Can I have everyone's attention? We have a plan if you'll just take a seat, we can start to figure this fucking nightmare out" I said

It took everyone a few minutes, but eventually, they calmed down and took a seat though some seemed like they were less than impressed with the fact I was the only one with any kind of plan. I went over attendance and then proceeded to explain our idea and what jobs we needed to be filled for the good of the group. First, we asked for volunteers, and when that didn't seem to work, we randomly assigned jobs to people considering that we had a couple of teachers in the group and a few guys who were straight-up workhorses. People were less than happy with that idea, so we allowed the people to trade jobs as needed. Then we talked about the rules or "laws" as we called them for group survival. All jobs had to be done to the maximum every day. If a job was not done, then the person responsible for not completing their job would be put on a water diet for one week. A second failure would result in a two-week diet of water. A third offense would result in that person being excommunicated from our group. If a person was excommunicated and found trying to get back onto the property or trying to steal from the group, they would be executed. The same laws and punishments applied to anyone caught stealing from another member of the group. We felt that these "laws," as we called them, would help keep the group from sitting on their hands while others worked for them and would help keep things going forward. I'm sure to others, it seems harsh, but we had to take drastic measures to make sure the group kept functioning smoothly. Instantly I had some push back from Robbie and my brother Carl. It was explained at this time that if anyone did not wish to stay, they did not have to. They could excommunicate themselves, and any further action on their part would result in immediate execution. The group didn't need the added stress caused by self-absorbed individuals.

After we broke from the meeting, both my wife and my ex-wife approached me, talk about the one thing on this earth that at that time, that could make me sweat and nervous.

"You didn't give either of us a job, so what the fuck are we going to do?" my wife said aggressively

I calmly told them both that they oversaw securing my children both at night and during the day. This less than amused my wife

"Why the fuck do you want that bitch helping me?" she growled.

"Honestly, I know that she will help you protect our children like they are her own, you need the backup, and sometimes you will need the break, and she will be there to help with that" I explained

This was not an argument my wife was going to win, and she knew that as she walked away, muttering under her breath about what a fucking asshole I am, at least that much had not changed.

We selected three people to run the radio job, three eight-hour shifts, and they started immediately so we might find out what caused all the chaos and possibly what was headed towards or away from our location. The property was eighty acres, and one mile down the road on one side lived my aunt at our pig farm on the opposite side of the road was our cow farm where my sister lived. They were both told to go home, and we sent a few group members down with them to live and help provide some security. My sister was beyond pissed over this because she wanted to be wherever my father was. It took my father speaking to her in private before she agreed to stay at her own house.

Everyone would meet at six o'clock for dinner every day. We were only eating one big meal per day to keep food rationed for extended periods. At this time, children, twelve and under, would eat first, then children thirteen to eighteen would eat, then the group elders which were fifty-five and older, then women, then adult males. At that time, the shooter aids would get food and take it to their assigned shooters in their shooting position. They would also sit and eat with the shooter for a few minutes of company and conversation.

We set up a shooting station at the corner of my road and the road the farms were on. By doing this, it gave us a good fire lane from there to just past the main headquarters to just past the farms in the event that we would have to start return fire. We set up another fire station on the backside of the property where Bravo team was set up.

The group was having a hard time adjusting at first to the new living arrangements. We only had five standing cabins, two farmhouses, and the main headquarters; in some cases, we had to put three families in one small ass cabin. People were fighting some, which we expected early on. Finally, people got a sleep rotation going in each cabin so that everyone could have a decent night's sleep on a bed, not just some on the bed and some on the floor, but everyone was getting a turn in a bed. People took to their jobs better than we had expected. On that end, it seemed like we were moving along as a community would.

The chatter over the short-wave radio was chaotic at best. There was no clear indication as to what caused the war to start. According to some unknown voices, it was the crazy whites who started shooting anyone who wasn't white. Other theories were that it was the government that began to attack the people, it was the far-left group Antifa, it was riots in the cities that escalated into war caused by the Black lives matter group. Islamic terrorism was at the top of other lists. It didn't matter to me how it all started. The question was, could it have been prevented? I'm sure it could have, but everyone was too busy fighting over who was right and not paying any attention to how it all went wrong. It's here now at our front door, all we can do is fight for one another or fight one another with any alliances we can make till it's over.

CHAPTER 4

It was mid-August, the group was doing well. Adjustments were made to jobs and housing to keep certain people away from others. We were starting to get a lot of extra firewood and water stockpiled. The canning of excess fruits, vegetables, and herbs was also piling up, and it was starting to look like we would make it through the first winter without a problem, until one day we awoke and the lights were no longer working.

Panic started spreading throughout the group. People were worried and began to whisper about EMPs. We again called everyone to the town hall. We assured them that it was not an EMP.

"How can you possibly know that" shouted my younger sister

I explained to everyone at that point if it was an EMP, our LED weapon lights and red dot optics on our guns would not work. Someone from the radio team went on to explain that there was chatter of an explosion at the central East Coast electrical hub in Virginia. There was, however, no definite group to blame for it.

The meeting broke, and things within the group started to settle down again. It was only a few days before that changed; however, then I get a call over the radio from Two-Five.

"Six-Eight, Six-Eight, this is Two-Five I need to see you at the pavilion immediately. How copy?"

"Good copy Two-Five I'm headed that way now," I said

When I arrived, Two-Five informed me that my brother and his wife were becoming an ever-increasing problem. He and his wife must have run out of whatever stash of drugs and the two-pack a day habit they had. Their ghetto attitudes were getting increasingly worse, and my brother was beginning to get hostile with everyone who came near him. His wife had started complaining of nausea and was extremely agitated. He's a work-horse his job was wood gathering. I put him in the back by Bravo team to keep him away from me. Honestly, every member of Alpha and Bravo teams were more brothers to me than him, and he was a constant thorn in my side my entire life.

Years before the war, I had planned for the unfortunate fact that my ghetto trash brother and his family would be near home or find their way home. I had started a footlocker full of pornographic magazines with the theory that when he started coming off the drugs and his two pack a day habit, he could take a magazine off by himself for some "alone time" to help combat his withdrawal.

I asked Two-Five to send One-Three with my brother and his wife to the pavilion, or the town hall as we liked to call it, so that I could remind them that we have rules in which we live by during this time and if they couldn't handle it, they were going to have to leave for the benefit of the group. When they got to the town hall, he started with his usual scumbag ghetto talk.

"Fuck you and your bullshit. I'll beat your ass, take your guns and fucking kill you, we don't have to do a fucking thing you say to us," he barked on his approach.

"You and your woman should bear in mind that I've been a student of violence for the better part of the last decade. Even if I started to lose, I'd get out one of the many cheat codes I keep on my person at any given time, I'll bleed you out, and as your dying, I'll make you watch as I gut that ghetto trash bitch you call a wife. Perhaps you should take a dirty magazine, go snap one or two off to help get your fucking shit together. Remember, there are five other guys on my team who have been begging since they arrived for me to give the order to take you off this fucking earth. Now take your brand of stupid and get the fuck out of my face before I give the god damn order, and have you killed."

I was interrupted by One-Three "Fucking."

"What?" I asked

"Fucking," replied One-three

"What about fucking?" I said with confusion on my face

You know, like in a movie. I'll have you FUCKING killed; it makes it sound more urgent," One-Three explained further

"You're such an asshole," I told him

One-Three raised his finger "fucking asshole!" with excitement on his face

It was at this time I understood where he was going with this. I turned and smiled at my brother, shaking my head as the two of them turned and walked away, muttering to each other I pulled One-Three close to me.

"You keep your god damn eyes on him, and if it needs to be done, then you fucking deal with it."

"Wilco boss," he replied, then he turned and disappeared into the woods.

Hours later, Doc tracked me down. He had my sister with him. I was guessing at this point that my brother had gone and complained to her about the way I had spoken to him and his wife. Like the ignorant person my sister can be, she went and complained to my father because hey, we have time for sibling stupidity acting like we're twelve instead of near thirty-one. You could see the anger in my sister's eyes as they approached.

"We need to talk about your attitude towards your brother and his wife," Doc said

Before he could say another word to me, I faced my sister

"I've got a six-man team of well-trained shooters protecting nearly one hundred people who are all here because this country is at fucking war with itself and god knows who else, I need mother fuckers to do the jobs assigned to them without fail so that the team and I can do our god damn jobs. I don't have time to babysit a near thirty-one-year-old and his bitch because instead of being productive members of society, they spent the last twelve years doing drugs and living off the system. If it means at the end of the day that I must give the order to end their lives to keep the rest of these people alive, then I certainly god damn will. Put the past twenty plus years of sibling rivalry aside. It's my job to keep everyone alive, pull your head out of dad's ass, keep our brother in check, and away from me so that this can go as smoothly as possible for everyone else. Also, you can take him and his cluster fuck family down to your house because I don't want to see his stupid ass around me again if I can avoid it, do you fucking understand me?" I said undoubtedly less than calmly.

Crying her eyes out, she yelled "yes" and ran off.

"That's not how a leader is supposed to deal with things," Doc said

"I'm not here to be a leader. I am here to keep everyone alive. You can by-all means deal with the petty shit, so I don't have to," I said as I turned towards him.

"Well, I think your plan is flawed, you need an observation post and a listening post at nighttime, this way you'll know if people were sneaking up on us or on their way to us," he suggested.

"We gave radios to the other farms on this road and surrounding roads; they are our long-distance eyes and ears," I explained to him.

"Well, I think if you and your Rambo want to be buddies, who seem to think you know it all, should each take ten people and go train them. Then I think you need to start sending people out to look for things, things like diesel fuel, trucks, abandoned tractors, more guns, ammo, reloading supplies and so forth" he said

"You want me to send people to their death?" I asked

"NO, we need more than what we have. The only way we are going to get the extras we need is to go looking for them," he barked.

"What the fuck do you think will happen when one of those people are seen in the scope of a local farmer, who is scared out of his mind, you think he won't pull the trigger on them? Do you seriously think for a moment that if we send people out to take from others that they will make it back here?" I asked in total disbelief

"No don't mean they should take from local farmers, we should be working with them, I mean, send them to Goldbeach" he barked at me

"OK!" I laughed, "So you want to send them into the biggest part of this war near us? That will not go any better than taking from farmers" I was still laughing

"You don't know what you're talking about" he shouted at me

"If you want to give up your small stockpile of guns and send a bunch of untrained monkeys out into that circus then you go ahead, you can be their leader, and YOU can take responsibility for when they do not come home" I shouted back

Doc walked away, pissed. He assembled a ten-man team that he sent out with a list of stuff to find. When they didn't come back after two weeks, he assembled another. When they didn't come home either, he didn't try again, and we never spoke of it after that.

In the following days, it seemed people were working together to get things done and, most importantly, getting along with each other. Things, of course, wouldn't stay that way forever. Our radio team put the call out that they needed me at Main, as soon as possible. Our radio team was a group of three people that sat by the short-wave radio twenty-four hours a day, three separate eight-hour shifts. Their job was to write down all the information that they heard and try their best to sort out the truth from all the lies. The best any of us could figure was if it came over the radio from what we could identify as three separate sources. The general information may be correct. An example of this came with what they had told me at that moment.

The Word was that the New York State Police was teamed up with the New York National Guard; however, the information after that was scattered at best. Some were saying that their job was to go door to door and confiscate weapons from citizens. Some were saying that they were simply going door to door to see if anyone needed medical transport or assistance. Other reports had them just solely on rolling patrol together. One thing for sure was that the fact they were working together was probably accurate.

More chatter suggested that every major city and many of the smaller towns were in full out war, it didn't appear at that time that it was anywhere near us, but I knew that wouldn't remain the case. After the gangs in the cities consumed every resource they could, they would eventually make their way towards us, one town at a time. Chatter did suggest that the small towns were not immune, however, to violence. Multiple home invasions, robberies, murders, and rapes were being reported in damn near every small town between the cities. We would surely see that attempt at action before we saw a significant threat in our area.

It was early-September when Robbie and Ann's husband Ryan approached me all sorts of pissed off.

"Why the fuck are we working our asses off while you and your buddies all sit around pretending like you're doing something special that the rest of us can't do?" Ryan said with a nasty tone.

"First off, ass clowns, we're not pretending to anything special, we've all spent a great deal of money and our personal time away from our families training to keep them safe. We all decided to live a lifestyle that keeps our heads on a swivel watching for the threats that you and your family pretended didn't exist while sitting in your bullshit world. That's why you're here. Because your wife, my ex-wife, knew that you'd be safe here. Because while you were out every Friday drinking with your buddies and having orgies, I was packing up my gear, headed to a class that gave me the training I would need to keep not only my family safe but the families of those around me safe. To be honest, I would let you two ass clowns help us if I thought for one second, you'd follow orders and not get my men killed. If we're not at our posts on our regular shifts, then some cock bag piece of shit could very easily slip in here rape and kill your family just like they almost did four months ago when I saved your sorry asses to fucking start with."

They certainly were not happy with my response as they turned and walked away, muttering to each other. It did, however, get me thinking that the teams were stretched thin, but I couldn't just throw a bunch of untrained people into the mix and expect anything positive to come of it. They were the very least of my current problems. However, dealing with the petty issues that were being forced on me was taking its toll. Without a doubt, I was getting agitated with everyone, whether they did something wrong or not. I looked at my watch, I had a full two hours before I was supposed to make my way to Alpha, so I decided to head to the cave for a cigar.

I was the only one down there, which was honestly a relief at that point, I grabbed a cigar from the humidor, and for the first time since this started, I even took the time to look at it before I cut and lit it. It was a Kentucky fire-cured by Drew Estate. The aroma of campfire and leather filled the room as I fired it up. This was probably the most relaxing moment I've had since June. It was quiet in the cave, a bit cool but calm. I walked around sipping on my canteen while puffing on my cigar, trying to organize some of the stuff we never got to. Rearranging the books on the shelf, moving cans of ammo around so that they were more neatly stacked, just then I heard the pitter-patter of little feet above my head and the voice of the most beautiful princess in the world and my handsome little man both yelling

"Daddy, are you in the basement?"

"Yes, I am," I responded, and they both came running down the stairs. They indeed broke the quiet I needed, but that was also the noise I needed the most. It was almost hard to believe how happy they were, innocent, they had no idea the world was falling apart around them, and they could care less. They ran back and forth, chasing each other while I watched and smiled. It was the best hour of this whole mess, but now I was done with my cigar and had to get ready to head to work.

"Dada, are you going to work?" my daughter asked.

"Yes, Princess, I am."

"Why, dada?"

"Because there are a lot of people here who depend on daddy and your uncles to keep them safe."

"Why dada?" as a typical three-year-old would ask yet again.

"Because grandpa said so, Princess." which my answer to her every time she would start the hundred "why daddy" questions.

"Oh ok." which was the answer I always got from her when I responded that way.

I gave my kids hugs and kisses, and off I went towards Alpha. Upon my arrival, Six-One had our camping French press out, making me a pot of coffee.

"How the fuck are you doing, brother? Anything I should be concerned with?" I asked.

"The assholes are driving my wife insane, and it's starting to cool off a lot lately, but otherwise, life is good." Explained Six-One, "No movement downrange and nothing worth talking about over the radio from either of the farms or surrounding lookouts."

"Roger that brother" as I took my first cup of freshly brewed coffee from Six-One

"How are you doing?" he asked as I sipped my brew "you seem drained, brother everything good with you?"

"Well, I had yet another much-expected incident with the scumbag and his ghetto trash bitch that, of course, I had to deal with, and of course my stupid ass sister had to put in her bullshit and cry to our father. Then Ann's dipshit brother and husband had to come to give me their opinion on how they think life should be going. OF COURSE, they feel they shouldn't have to do much of shit other than being on vacation. Yes, brother, I'm damn tired, and I'm worried that my plan may not be the best thing for the group."

"From the very first time you told me what the plan would be, it sure seemed to me like you had your shit together. I remember telling my wife that if it ever came to it, I knew you would keep my family safe as if they were your own. You treated us like we were family from day one. I'll never forget how blown away Sarah was when you and the boys came to the hospital after that accident I was in. She could not believe how fast you guys were there for us. I know that is not the same as what is happening here today, but damn brother, we are two months into this shit, and you have managed to keep everyone busy, everyone involved in what is happening, you are doing the very best you can with all things considered. I put my family's life in your hands because I believe in your plan and god damn brother, I believe in your ability to lead this team I love you brother, and I have your back" Six-One explained with what looked to be tears in his eyes

"I love you too brother," I told him as I sat back putting my feet up "You make good coffee too bitch"

He burst out laughing. That is just how we all were. We couldn't have a serious conversation with each other at all without insulting or name-calling.

"Hey, did I ever tell you about my meatus?" Six-One said with a shit-eating grin on his face

"I'm sure this is not something I want to hear, but we are stuck here for the next few, so you may as well tell me now" as I sipped my coffee

With the most serious look on his face, Six-One began, "So, you remember the car accident I was in last year. I was in the emergency room with that neck brace on in the most pain I have ever been in when the nurses started cutting off my clothes. Well, one of them, after getting my pants off, walked over and started handling my junk and she says to the doctor that there was no major bleeding around the meatus, which even with all the pain I was in, I took to mean there was some bleeding and I screamed out what the fuck is wrong with my meatus!!!"

That was seriously the wrong story to tell as I sipped my coffee. I spit it out everywhere I was laughing so hard, which was just what I needed from him the most, a good laugh.

Just then, a call came over the radio from Two-Eight that my attention was needed at Main immediately. I got up quickly and ran back to the house as fast as I could to find my wife and my ex-wife in a brawl with each other over God only knows what. Two-Eight and I pulled them off each other, I told my wife to go into the house that I would be in soon, and I told Ann to wait her happy ass right there, that I would be out to get her side of it soon enough.

"What the fuck is your god damn problem," I shouted as I walked into the house. "Seriously is there not enough problems going on at this moment?"

"Remember when you said our princess got her blonde hair and blue eyes because you cheated on me with a blonde hair blue eyed woman?" my wife rambled off.

Before she could finish rambling, her unique batch of stupid, "Are you fucking kidding me right now?" I said laughingly

She started back in, "Well, I just realized your ex has blonde hair and blue eyes, and I see how she fucking looks at you. I always knew you cheated on me."

Once again, I interrupted her, "I recall telling you years ago that I was done defending myself to your particular brand of stupid. There is far more important shit going on here, don't you think? Your bullshit will take a back seat, and this will not happen again. HOW FUCKING CLEAR AM, I?"

She responded with what I determined years before was one of her programmed responses when she was wrong "whatever."

"Don't fucking whatever me!! There are one hundred people here counting on my ability to lead my shooters and keep them safe from the world outside of here. If they see my house in disarray, tell me how the fuck they will have any kind of confidence that I can do my job. Tell me now if I fucking need to speak any god damn slower or in crayon for you to understand me?"

"No, I fucking understand, asshole," she yelled as she stormed off pissed as a fart.

I turned and walked outside to ask Ann her side of what happened. "You want to tell me what the fuck you did to cause all that shit to happen?" I asked

"All I did was ask your princess where she got her pretty blonde hair and blue eyes from, all of a sudden, your bat shit crazy wife started yelling at me, calling me a whore and attacked me," she said, still trying to catch her breath.

I started laughing and told her I would maybe explain what happened to her someday when life was back to normal, but until then, she would just have to wonder and leave that question alone. I turned and started walking back to the firing station laughing to myself some and in the same breath plotting my wife's death. I mean, I wouldn't really kill her, but god damn how much stupid have I already had to put up with, and now she's adding her own god damn brand.

As I drew closer to Alpha, I could see Six-One on the bolt gun just then he came over the radio

"Boss, I need you back here and god damn fast, we got a big problem."

CHAPTER 5

We received word over the radio that there was some serious trouble headed our way. There was a white Ford cargo type van with a driver and at least one passenger. We had received reports earlier of a vehicle matching that description driving around robbing homes, murdering anyone who tried to stop them. With almost one hundred percent certainty, we knew they would probably attack our farm because everyone in the damn county knew we raised animals for food and profit. It was a lucky day for them. They were finally going to meet some guys that would match the fight they put forth.

I pulled Six-One instantly to go with me to the farmhouses. I told Two-Eight to get on the bolt gun until Two-Five could get to Alpha and provide cover for us. We hauled ass to the farms making movement down both sides of the road using the tree line as cover in case the van got there before we did. Upon our arrival, we told everyone to hide in the basements of the houses.

I told Six-One to set up on the northeast corner of our calf barn while I took a position on the northwest corner of our hay barn. We were both roughly twenty yards from the road. I threw a small sand sock into the road. The plan was when the van hit that spot. We would shoot out the front tires of the van as close to the same time as possible. This would make it hard for the people in the van to pinpoint exactly where the shots came from and how many of us there were.

I radioed to Six-One as the van came into our line of sight "fire in three, two, one."

Our shots broke, hitting both front tires. The van started swerving. The driver managed to keep control of the van keeping it on the road bringing it to a stop. Instantly the driver and passenger exited the van, armed with what looked to be AKs. Eight more guys exited the back of the van armed as well. The way they fumbled around told us many things. First being that they had no real weapons training at all, and secondly being they showed up not expecting a fight like the one we were about to give them. They were shouting at each other, trying to figure out where the shots had come from, by looking at them, they were probably meth cookers from one of the nearby trailer parks.

They honestly never even stood a chance. Six-One and I shot four of them, each with two direct center mass hits. The other two guys were dead before they even hit the ground with a really lovely shot to the face from about a half-mile out. This was a tell that Two-Five was on the bolt gun at Alpha.

"Nice shooting Two-Five," I said over the radio

"Not bad considering I was aiming for his chest." replied Two-Five

"Fuck, that asshole always gets lucky with his hits," yelled Six-One

Team protocol was now to remove all weapons, ammunition, and any documents that could indicate if these skinnies were attached to any local groups operating in the area. Or indicating where exactly they might be from, so we know more about who is operating nearby. Once we gathered all the things, we needed we moved the van down the road a little way down and parked it sideways in the road, obstructing as much of the road as we could so in the off chance someone else comes for a fight, they'd be forced through the opening we have allowed them with their vehicles.

Six-One and I split up between the farmhouses alerting everyone that they could come out of hiding and resume normal activities. I instructed my brother to feed the bodies of the recently departed to the pigs, which should hold the pigs over for several days. Six-One and I headed back to Alpha. I told Two-Eight that he was in charge and to keep Three-Three from sitting in the fetal position for the rest of his life. Since the fight was over for now. Team protocol had more for us to do, Six-One, Two-Five, and I headed from there to Main.

We all made our way down to the cave, Six-One and I both grabbed cigars while Two-Five poured all three of us a small glass of bourbon. We all sat filling out incident reports. If the war ever ended, people would need to know what happened, and like law enforcement had to before this, we felt it in our best interest to do the same. Our reports included every detail from the incident, including radio chatter during the event itself, all events after including make model and serial numbers of all the weapons we gathered off the dead, as well as the make, model, and vin off the van. Team protocol stated a mandatory break from duty after a critical incident, which included one drink, one cigar or pipe, and four hours with our feet up.

As we sat going over the documents recovered from the van, Six-One alerted me to the registration. It was a Glodbeach address. Moments later, Two-Five unfolded a small piece of notebook paper that had our location address on it. The best we could guess at this moment was that one of the guys Doc sent off to get "supplies" was caught and possibly tortured for information as to where he came from. Some of the documents recovered suggested that they were not meth cookers either, but they were attached to the white supremacy movement in some way. This explained why they drove past everyone else and came right for us. How many other fights would we have because of those who never came back?

Reports filled out, Two-Five and I played a couple of games of chess with the rest of our free time, while Six-One started a book he picked from the team library. We all were quiet at this point. Even as it got closer to head back on duty, my heart was still racing a bit. None of us wanted this, but what else were we going to do, pray someone else would help us? With downtime ending, we all got up, put our gear back on, resupplied what ammo we use. Then took two of the AKs we collected, function checked them, grabbed half of the magazines, and headed back to Alpha.

Upon my arrival, Two-Eight gave me a quick update on the absolutely nothing that happened while I was gone, except that he didn't think Three-Three was doing so well. Two-eight left and headed to Main when I turned around to see Three-Three still sitting there where he was when I left. It didn't look like he had moved except maybe to puke.

"Are you having some issues, brother?" I asked

"Yeah a few goddamn more than twelve" you could hear the fear in his voice

"What the fuck happened in the last five hours that has your silly ass still shaking? You had company while I was gone, did Two-Eight refuse to whisper sweet nothings in your ear or something?" I laughed

"You know what, fuck you!!!!" he shouted, "I'm not like you guys. I mean, seriously, how the fuck can you guys just run down there kill however many people you did then come back here like you just went out for tacos at the titty bar?"

"Honestly, brother, I had no clue how the fuck anyone of us was going to react to what just happened. At this point, I don't believe any of us have even dealt with the fact we just killed those men in our heads. I don't believe any of us will either. We can't, too many people's lives depend on our ability to do our fucking job. In July, I was faced with a possible situation. I was shaking so fucking bad I just knew if I had to, it would have brought half the city down on my position. Still, at that time, I was also alone and trying not to draw any attention to myself so that I could make it home to my family. Several hours into my journey home, I shot three guys and cut another's throat to save lives and again to make it home. Now I'm here, and it's my duty to protect not just them but your family as well. Today was about keeping all the people here alive that's why we moved down and took the fight to them before they could bring it to us. That's why we set up a block of time for team guys to decompress after such an incident, so we don't lose our shit later while we're on duty. We do what we do for you, our families, your family, and the people here." I explained

"Then why the fuck am I shaking so bad? Why the fuck was I puking earlier? I didn't do shit earlier except sit here. I didn't even watch what you guys did. Yet here I am, I'm supposed to be one of you guys" he sobbed

"You are one of us. You're just not like us. We trained, competed in the shooting sports, focused on building the mindset to prepare us for a real shitty situation. You're losing your shit because your subconscious knows that if the team and I had failed in our mission that you were going to have to pick up a gun and fight in our place. You believe if that had happened, you and many of our family would have died, and it makes you sick, thinking you would have failed in your mission." I said

"I'm not trained for this shit like you guys, I didn't think this could ever happen remember, I thought you were fucking nuts getting ready for a war that couldn't possibly happen," he said

"It was never just about a war on American soil. It was about being trained and willing to do whatever I had to do to protect my family because it's my job; it always has been. You, however, believed someone else would protect your family. That's why you went on in your life, pretending that the world was not the sick, scary fucked up place it is. I'm going to train you for the fight, brother, I'm going to make you ready, so if the fight comes to you, you will be able to destroy those that intend us harm. You will be able to fight not just for your family but mine as well." I explained as I lit a cigar, "it's time we put this shit past us, man the fuck up and accept the world never was what you believed it to be, and if this shit ever ends, it will never be what it was before" I explained as I puffed on my cigar.

The team was on edge after the incident, every sound making us look just a bit deeper into the woods, a bit further past the farms. The group went on like nothing had happened like it was headline news that was no longer headlining their lives. I was gearing up one day and overheard some conversation between two of our residents.

"That will not happen again. This is a small town; everyone now knows what will happen if they come here looking for a fight," they said.

Unfortunately, this is not the same small town it once was, people hiding in their homes or at a friend's house for safety. They're not going to the store or the local bar anymore to talk about the local gossip. Not to mention the fact that yes, we won that fight and yes, people know it, the worry now is that others will come for that fight just to see what they can get, that they may not have.

It was about a week after the first critical incident. I had just come off shift and now had twelve hours of downtime before I had to return to work. I found Ann and asked her to keep a close eye on my kids for a while so that I may have what was beyond needed alone time with my wife. I tracked her down, and we very quickly snuck off to the bedroom. Once in the room, we were kissing very passionately, with much aggression taking each other's clothes off as it had been so many months since we had the chance. I threw her naked onto the bed kissing on her body, biting at her flesh as I craved her like I never had before, pushing her legs apart climbing between then I started to push my way inside her when all of a sudden our bedroom door burst open

"Oh, fuck shit, boss god damn, I'm sorry," Three-Three shouted as he turned his back to us.

"What the miserable fuck do you god damn want" I barked as I stood up off the bed, grabbing my pants.

"Two-Eight was trying to get you on coms. There is a car coming up the road west of Alpha," he said in a panic.

I immediately finished getting dressed, threw on my chest rig, grabbed my shotgun, headed downstairs, out of the house fast, and to the end of the driveway. Upon my arrival, I could see a car parked two hundred yards from my driveway. The driver then stepped out, waving his hands around in the air. He was just out of a reasonable range for my shotgun with slugs. I radioed to Two-Five he was already on the scope, ready to fire if given the order as the man was right around a thousand yards from Alpha. The man started walking closer, still waving his arms in the air. He was roughly fifty yards away when he shouted

"I'm a loser baby, so why don't you kill me!!!!!" he then turned and walked back to his car. I radioed to Two-Five to stand down as this guy was friendly. The words shouted were the lyrics of an old song I remember from high school. We had given this line to people we were close to whom lived far away. If the area they lived in ever got too hot for them to survive, they needed just to remember those words as they got close to us. No matter which team member they came across, those words would be their ticket into our area of operation.

I waved the man forward; he got into his car and drove to us. He stepped out of his car, and to my surprise, it was an old friend of the family, a man we called the Angry Midget or Midge for short. At a staggering five foot three inches tall and honestly one of the happiest people you would ever meet, not much brought the man down. At one-time, Midge was one of my best friends, but we slowly grew apart because I began to believe that a trained fighter with one gun was more reliable than an untrained fighter with one hundred guns. He, however, did not feel as I did. As I took to the range, spending my money to train with the best instructors I could, he spent his money on more and more guns. When New York passed the "Safe Act," Midge began looking for work in the field he was already in just outside of the state. He finally found such work. Only his wife decided she and the children would not be traveling with him. Since his family didn't follow him, he had fallen down a lousy path. It didn't take long, however, for him to find comfort in God. He had become an ordained priest and was preaching on Sundays at the local church where he now lived. We started helping him to unload his car, which he had filled with a massive stock of ammunition AR and AK rifles, even a few belt-fed semiautomatic browning 1919s. He was certainly a sight for sore eyes, not only because he brought us much needed fire support but also because I figured his work as a preacher might help some of the group who may still not be coping with the changes very well.

We finished unloading his car. He started going over the use, cleaning, and clearing malfunctions in the 1919's. Both of which were headed to the firing stations, as soon as the guys could learn how invaluable these tools were going to be for us. After a few hours, we spread the word that we would now have a priest for Sunday morning church services and for anyone who may need his council or council in the lord. His presence certainly seemed to have an incredibly positive effect on a lot of the group in the days to follow, which I must say was a massive relief on myself and the rest of the team.

My wife was at this point not speaking to me because after Midge's arrival, we never did finish the alone time we had started, well right away anyway, we did get the chance again about a week later, and it was worth the wait. It had only been a few minutes after we had finished, both of us laying there talking a little, our sweaty bodies still holding each other close that there was a knock on our bedroom door.

"Um, boss, I hate to interrupt again, and I'm hoping that you guys are not just getting started" Three-Three was stuttering from the other side of the door. "But I just got word that we have company coming from east of Alpha, and your presence is requested immediately."

My wife just laughed, honestly. I think that may have been the first time she had laughed in a long time, "Just go," she said. "I got what I wanted," she laughed. I got dressed, grabbed my gear as I had before, and made my way down to Alpha, where Two-Eight was waiting for me. He began to tell me he was sure, looking through the spotting scope, that he recognized one of the men in the rather large group that was approaching our position. I took one look in the scope and was immediately excited. As members of the last school, I trained in hand-to-hand combat were making their way closer with one of the most magnificent and most inspirational people I had ever met leading the pack.

Richard was his name; he had his arms high in the air, waving a team challenge coin that he had been given by me the year prior. He didn't necessarily believe war could ever happen as it had. But, once had asked me if it ever did if he and his family could come down for their safety. I, of course, said yes and gave him a team challenge coin that he could give to any team member, and they would know he was good people. Richard was a few years younger than me and hugely successful. He worked in a prosthetics lab before the main event. He was married and a father of three. He had a more natural talent in him than in anyone I ever met before. Truly gifted, he spent almost all his life learning various martial arts, and the near-decade that I had known him, he was an instructor, as a side job, teaching various hand-to-hand and Krav Maga classes. He started learning Brazilian Jiu-jitsu within six months he took home a gold medal in his belt class at a local competition.

He arrived with about forty other people, including his wife and children. Several of the people with him were students at the last school he was teaching at. One other person with him was a woman named Robin. She was in her early forties, five foot ten inches tall, long blonde hair, incredibly intoxicating blue eyes. She was as well an instructor at the school I had last trained at. Probably the first woman I ever met with all I can describe as a true warrior spirit. I was pleased to see that she had met up with Richard and made her way down to safety. I was unaware in that moment just how much of a pain in my ass her warrior spirit was going to be.

We sent anyone who needed any kind of medical attention to see Doc and the EMTs. We assigned everyone a place where they could sleep, a job, and explained how everything worked around here to keep everything going while the world fell around us. After helping everyone get settled, Richard and I sat at the town hall chatting for a little while to catch up. He told me the group had been a bit larger when they left their homes approximately sixty miles north of our position. A few people decided not to continue after the death of several others who had decided to make the journey as well. They had encountered some skinnies along the way, got into a few gunfights, which was how some were killed. He believed two had died en route due to dehydration. We talked family for a few more minutes. That's when he decided to ask if my fat ass was doing anything to stay in shape. I was informed he would like to start a training program so that he could continue teaching as he had been. This would help him to adjust to the new life that was laid out in front of him.

It was at that moment I realized the answer to a problem we had as a group just arrived literally at my doorstep. I told Richard I would discuss this more with him later and instantly radioed to Two-Five telling him to meet me in the cave. I had just lit a cigar when he came walking down, throwing his chest rig to the floor and setting his KSG on the pool table.

"What's up brother," he asked

"You haven't met Richard before today; however, you have heard of him before. He was one of my instructors at the school where I got my black belt and the man who pushed me the most to earn it before he started teaching at the other school I started going to before my shoulder injury. What's your thoughts on using our new guests to train new team members in hand-to-hand combat as well as extreme fitness training. At the same time, you and I teach weapons familiarization and manipulation to the same group of volunteers so that we can expand the team beyond two firing teams?" I asked

"I think that's probably the best idea you had since this whole mess started, boss, especially since you still won't let me shoot your brother," he said with a chuckle.

"Brother, you really need to let that shit go," I told him with a smile.

CHAPTER 6

The morning had come before Two-Five, and I had completed what would become the first standards for the new team member training program. It was also determined that current team guys would as well be required to train with the new trainees. We can't expect people to train if we are not training ourselves. I walked outside to find that we had our very first heavy snowfall. It was almost a peaceful feeling to see the way the snow covered the ground and the trees, made me forget for a moment all the hell we had been through, and what hell was to come. It was calming.

This was the point, other than keeping track of making sure regular duties had been completed and that my children were in school, that I got the sense that everyone would stay in their current homes; instead of roaming around trying to find stuff to keep themselves busy. Unfortunately, this would also be the start of some of the hardest times for us. We would still have to be cutting firewood regularly. However, the wood must be rationed as much as possible due to not being able to cut every day. Other team members and I would use less wood than other people in the group because we had prepared for this, we had cold weather gear suitable for long days on over-watch. Sickness and hypothermia were still going to be significant concerns, especially with our elderly.

I finally shook off the beauty and the fear of what this weather could bring. I got Richard and Robin to meet me at the town hall. Upon their arrival, I broke out the blueprints that Two-Five and I had come up with. Of course, now it was time for their input. Richard suggested that we have two, three-hour blocks of hand-to-hand combat and fitness instruction. This would make it possible for all current team members to make at least one training session per day. Richard suggested that we also do a weapons training program for the new guys. He had come to me a few times prior for training himself, so he knew the knowledge would be suitable for others. Fortunately, Two-Five and I had already planned for that. We designed the weapons training as a one-hour block twice a day immediately following the hand-to-hand and fitness class. I would teach one of the weapons classes, Two-Five would teach the other. This would also give us the chance to "refresh" ourselves on proper weapons handling, unorthodox shooting positions, use of lights, and malfunctions. We decided not to do anything live fire, due to needing every round of ammo we had for any possible bad situation that may come our way. Once again, if trainees were going through it, then so were current team guys. I know I'd lost some weight I'd most certainly also lost some of the edge I had worked so hard to gain. Current team members were required to attend one three-hour block of physical training and one block of firearms training. Trainees would be required to make only one block of physical training and both blocks of weapons training. After the first thirty days, we would select team captains from the trainees, at which time we would also start testing everyone on their abilities to see who would make it on to one of the teams. Trainees would immediately start taking part on shifts with current team members. They would take the place of the shooter's aids.

Two-Five disappeared into the woods looking for volunteers while I walked around the front of the property, looking for the same. We were looking for men ages eighteen to forty-five, and that was where I ran into my first big snag. When Robin found out we were looking for men to fight, she pitched a massive fit.

"What the fuck makes any man here better than me? If I'm good enough to train them then god damn it, I'm fucking good enough to fight alongside them!" she barked loudly as she walked towards me

"Robin listen it's not that I don't think you can fight as good if not better, seriously I've watched you in training, it's just that we are looking for fighters" but before I could finish that thought

"Stop with that chivalrous bullshit, I don't give a fuck that you would hold the door for me at class before all this happened, now things have changed, and if I'm going to train your fighters then I'm going to fight alongside you as well, besides I've seen some of the slack-jawed pussies that are getting in line to get trained and I could outfight all of them" she abruptly interrupted

She certainly had a valid point. We gathered everyone in the town hall, asking for volunteers. We got all of twelve from the hundred-plus that was amongst us. Robin, Ryan, Robbie, and Three-Three were among the twelve we got. Team members then got to select from the group two trainees that would stick to their sides like glue, even on shift. Since Three-Three was already on my hip ninety-nine percent of the time, he was a natural first pick, and before I could select another, I was interrupted

"I know you; I don't know anyone else, so if you think for a god damn second, I'm going to be placed with anyone except you, you're out of your god damn mind" Robin started in again

"Robin, you were going to be my second choice had you let me finish my selection. However, you had better understand right now that I am the one in charge of this team, I will not be constantly interrupted because you feel the need for your word to be heard over anyone else's. If you feel that for some reason, you will not have to follow the same orders as everyone else, you're dead wrong, and you can remove yourself right now. Am I understood?" I asked

She nodded with a smile on her face.

I instructed Robin and Three-Three to meet me at Main. Once they were gone, I told Two-Five that he needed to take Robbie and told Six-One that he needed to take Ryan. I felt it was in the group's best interest to keep them separated; they both agreed. I left the selection process and met up with my selected trainees. We met in the cave to go over the weapons they would use and the gear that they should consider using. We then left there and went up to Alpha to go over regular daily routines, which Three-Three was familiar with; however, he was going to have a lot more responsibilities than he previously had. I sent Robin off as her shift as a team member didn't begin till morning.

Training began the next day, officially with the first-class being weapons instruction. Midge started our weapons class with the overall function of the 1919 belt-fed weapons. He broke the instruction down to the essential basics, function, malfunction clearing, loading, and overall maintenance. After thirty minutes, he got out his AR rifles where I took over. We discussed handguns next, making sure everyone could breakdown the pistol they brought or were given. We then covered proper grip, stance, sight alignment sight picture, and proper reloading procedures.

Once that was over, we moved over to fitness and hand-to-hand combat training. It was an extremely exhausting class for me. I mean, it had been two years since my fat ass had been on the mat training. It was going to be interesting to see how the team guys that had never been through what I had reacted to the training.

I got about two hours of playtime with my kids before my shift started, and damn was I already sore. Upon my arrival at Alpha, I saw Robin and Three-Three were already there. Six-One and his crew were gathering their things to head back to Main. I again went over the procedures for the positions overwatch duties, which included watching for and making notes on any movement seen no matter how small, if it was of significant concern, radio to the rest of the team immediately. I explained that even though we now have a belt-fed weapon, the bolt gun is still our most valuable asset due to its ability to reach out further and more accurately. I also explained that it was not as simple as just point and shoot, that only three of the team guys even had any kind of experience with precision rifle shooting. I explained now that the team was a bit bigger, we could split the shift into threes so we would each have a small amount of downtime to help keep our sanity together.

"Why with all of these new-found semi-auto weapons you didn't have before and further that you're teaching us to use are you still using a shotgun?" asked Robin

"Black Betty and I have a lot of history, several firearms training courses together, and a lot of competitive shoots with her as well. Here at Alpha, I choose the bolt gun as my go-to weapon. However, if I must leave here to move to the farm or back towards Main, Black Betty is a force multiplier. My ability to use buckshot or my preferred slugs adds a unique level of devastation with each pull of the trigger. The sound of the twelve-gage and the devastation it does to the human body also adds a unique psychological effect on the enemy. If we can react in the same manner as we have already proven we can. This weapon is just as effective as the rifles you guys were given. In my opinion, you guys were given the easiest weapons to learn how to use. Some team guys switched over to the shotgun when this state passed the Safe Act, and since this shit started, they went back to the rifles they love. I am going to stick to using Black Betty, for, at this time, she has not let me down" If I had a better way to explain it to them, I would have but, it made sense to me.

Three-Three and Robin went through the paces of over-watch as I sat and observed, sipping on my coffee. Looking at them work, I was more confident than I had been before that this was the right decision.

The shift was over Two-Eight, and his crew showed up to relieve us.

"Want to partner up at tomorrows classes brother?" asked Two-Eight

"Absolutely brother" I responded

We did the typical bro hug and off my group, and I went back to Main. I instantly went right to my bedroom for some shut-eye. I had stripped my gear and was starting to undress when my wife walked in. She asked if I thought things were going to work out with new trainees helping us on over-watch. Honestly, I just wanted to sleep at that point, and I'm guessing she could tell because she just turned and walked out of the room, closing the door in a rather aggressive manner. She knew I was tired, and I understood her attempt to try to make things normal in an unnormal situation, but with five hours of training in the morning then an eight-hour shift on over-watch, I needed rest.

After some uncomfortable sleep, I awoke, geared up, gave my family hugs and kisses, and made my way to classes. This became normal for the next two weeks when we found our way to our next set of problems.

It was the third week in November when Richard pulled me aside after Two-Eight, and I had finished with morning classes before I could head down to Main and get changed.

"Will, I hate to have to tell you, but I figured this needs your attention. I'm noticing that some of the team guys and trainees are lacking in their training, not putting in nearly as much effort as they should" he told me

"That is an issue to say the very least, the look on your face, however, tells me you already have a plan to combat that shit," I said

"Remember when you were training, how every thirty days you would be tested on what you learned that month, then every three months you got tested on what you had learned over the last two months?" asked Richard

I nodded

"I'm thinking if we do that and structure it as a pass or fail, it would start motivating the guys to put in more work," Richard explained.

"That would help weed out the weak and determine how bad they genuinely want to be on the teams. We certainly are not elite US special forces, but we are the best we have, and we should expect the best from our people. Brief Robin as to the changes we have discussed. I want her to keep her eyes on current team guys while you watch the new guys," I explained.

I briefed the team over the radio as to the changes we had decided to make.

The cycle continued, only now everyone knew what was at stake, if you pass, you pass, if you fail, you can try again. After that, if you fail, you are cut from the teams. I had got word from our instructor team that most of everyone was starting to push a lot harder. Day in and day out, the cycle continued, teach, train, over-watch, sleep, and repeat. As the snow continued to fall, we got another serious workout daily, as we were forced to snowshoe to the firing stations and let me tell you when the snow fell harder, and the wind picked up, that was one horrible half-mile hike. Every day before, our first test was nasty as far as the weather was concerned.

The testing day arrived. I waited for Two-Eight to finish his over-watch shift as he had become my everyday training partner. We headed outback and began our testing. Testing was just as stringent as I remembered, but I passed. Two-Eight passed as well, and again he was much older than the rest of us, so I asked Richard to make his scores "the lowest standard" allowed. Ryan, Robbie, and Two-Five tested with us as well. Ryan passed barely, Robbie did not, he tried hard, but he still had more weight to lose before he would be able to keep up with what was required of him. Two-Five did not even finish his test. He could not handle the extreme physical requirements. I told him to meet me in the cave in thirty minutes.

I was already in the cave when Two-Five came down the stairs, he was pissed.

"I don't know why I fucking have to test, I'm Bravo team leader, I already have my position on this team, and I also helped you start this fucking team. This bullshit not only doesn't matter to me it's also not going to apply to me" he barked as he walked closer to me

"The rules apply to everyone, especially the team guys, and especially to the leaders of this team. You knew after the Shiv Works class we did you had this problem. You told me for a year straight; you were going to get your ass into a gym of sorts and start fight training to build your endurance. It's obvious you didn't do that. Seals, Rangers, and SWAT all train, all the time, and either they make the cut, or they get cut. We implemented testing so that guys who wanted to fight with us would not get us killed. We need to make sure everyone earns it. You understand me, brother?" I asked

"Well guess what, it's not up to you so take your testing and fuck off with it, I'm going back to Bravo and getting ready for my watch" he again yelled as he stormed out of the cave

Unfortunately, he did have a valid point. To remove someone from the team, I would need the team to vote for it to happen. I then radioed to all team members from both teams to see if they felt the trainees could handle over-watch for an hour or less. Once it was confirmed that the trainees could handle it, I told all team members, including Two-Five, to meet me in the cave as soon as all trainees were in position. Two-Five walked down the stairs to find us all sitting, we each decided to pour a glass of bourbon, Six-One and myself had lit a cigar.

"Well let's get this party started" stated Two-Five with a grin on his face

"This isn't that kind of party, brother; I'm calling for a team vote. We had rules from the very beginning, rules that effected the group and rules for the team during this shitty situation. As things have developed here in ways we could not have imagined, you and I made a decision that benefited the team by expanding it with the people who arrived seeking our protection. ONLY if they trained to our standards, however, would they be part of the team," I was explaining.

"Yeah I fucking remember" interrupted Two-Five

"Brother you need to let him finish," said One-Three

"How can we expect anyone to obey the rules we put in place if we do not live by them? I'm asking the four members of the team sitting here to vote on this. I can't vote as I am the one bringing this to the table, Two-Five can't vote as this directly affects him. Six-One, One-three, Six-Six, and Two-Eight, if we as sitting team members cannot pass or finish the testing, we require the trainees to pass should we be removed from our rank in the chain of command and ultimately removed from our position on the team?" I asked.

"Yes" replied Two-Eight and Six-one

"I do not see how we can expect the trainees to meet a standard if we do not meet the same. Our core as a team must be built on a solid foundation, so yes," replied Six-Six.

"Two-Eight's scores were what you determined to be the lowest standard, and he is going to vote against me? That is fucking bullshit," shouted Two-Five.

"He is twenty years older than you and almost twenty-five years older than Six-One. Both of them had the same score. You have no excuse for not finishing, especially when you knew you had an endurance problem."

When suddenly "Yes," said One-Three with a big sigh, "We cannot expect any standard except the one we as a team live by, brother," he explained.

"As of this moment for the next thirty days, you WILL go to both hand to hand training classes per day plus you will still teach your weapons class, and you will not hold your post on over-watch. At the end of the thirty days, if you do not pass, you will lose your rank as Bravo team leader. If you can't pass thirty days after that, you will lose your callsign patch and be removed from the team until you prove otherwise," I stated.

Two-Five walked out of the room, pissed. I then turned to One-Three and told him he would be temporarily in command of Bravo team, giving him the private channel that Two-Five and I used to communicate on. I proceeded to say to him and Six-Six that they would be splitting up his trainees and that they would have to pull twelve-hour shifts until his return to duty. I sent the team to take care of their duties. I grabbed a Perdomo twentieth anniversary cigar from the humidor with the hopes the rich, creamy smoke would help relax my mind after such a long day.

CHAPTER 7

It was December 23rd when we got our most substantial snowfall to date. I swapped out my usual chest rig for a plate carrier, the plates and soft armor in my mind would help keep me just a little bit warmer, especially with the temperature continuing to drop. More wood was taken to the firing stations, cabins, town hall, and Main. Before that, we had only been keeping enough at one place to last roughly twenty-four hours. The decision was now made to hold two weeks' worth all the time until spring. People would still need to be a bit conservative with their supply. The last thing we wanted was people getting sweaty because then they take off layers, which we all know leads to people getting sick. It's not like we can just run down to the local CVS for cough and cold medicine anymore.

People were, however, already starting to get sick, nothing major at the time, just some common colds. We took extra special attention to our elders, taking extra blankets to them. I even gave up some of my heavier socks to them to ensure they stayed warm. We made a bunch of rice bags so people could heat them as needed. Things moved forward, as usual, kids still went off to classes, team guys and trainees even went to their classes, and of course, everyone was again doing very well at their jobs.

Radio chatter was still minimal. The police band channels had been silent for too long. The best guess was that most law enforcement went home to protect their own families, or they were dead. There was still the occasional sighting of what was believed to be national guard troops but nothing of significant concern since the early reports.

I sat the next morning, sipping my coffee when my wife walked in. She told me that she had asked Robert to watch the kids after class because her, Ann, and Richard's wife were all going to head up the hill to Amish country. They were going to see what they could find for all the children from the Amish store for Christmas. I was a bit more tired that morning, so I raised my cup to her on her way out the door.

I let Two-Five do most of the instruction as I drank my second cup of coffee. We moved on to classes from there, I asked Two-Five if he would like to partner up, and to my surprise, he said yes. He didn't say very much during the class, but he did train hard. I took my usual short break after class, which, for me, meant spending time with my kids. On my way to Main, I passed Robert walking with my princess. I asked where they were going. My princess told me they were going for a walk, and they would be back in a little bit. When I got to Main, I saw my son busy playing with Six-One's "assholes," as he liked to call them. I decided since my children were otherwise occupied, it might be a good time to start packing up the majority of my gear so it could be moved up to the firing station. I figured with the extra harsh weather upon us. It would be best to keep all my gear there and sleep there as well, which spawned another idea which may or may not have been a good one. I radioed to One-Three for his opinion. The idea being that since we had such inclement weather, perhaps all team members and trainees should bunk at their perspective firing stations since it would be hard for off duty people to make it to a firing station in an emergency.

"Logic tells us there should be little to no movement during the big snow belt season, which is why we should be staying at the stations during this time," One-Three told me.

Logic also told us that by now, the cities that had been overrun were probably far low on resources, so there was still a high possibility that we could see some problems come down from there. However, we were not going to move anything until after Christmas.

CHAPTER 8

We awoke the next morning to screaming kids jumping on the bed. "It's Christmas!!!" they both were shouting before I could even open my eyes.

We made our way downstairs, telling the kids they would have to wait until we had coffee in our hands before we opened presents. The coffee was taking way too long that morning to brew with the kids losing their minds that early.

Richard and his wife walked downstairs not long after; I'm guessing by the look on their faces they were woke in the same manner that we were. I held out a coffee mug to Richard.

"You guys don't have any cream; I can't drink that shit black like you do." He said yawning

"I guess with all of your talents, being a man isn't one of them," I said, laughing as I sipped from my cup.

We gathered in the living room as others started to arrive. Everyone who could make it to Main did; my grandparents were going to stay at their cabin, as were others. My wife had plans to take the kids to see my grandparents when everything settled down for the day. Robert and Ann made their way up for the festivities as well. This year, of course, was different. The kids didn't get the latest new toys or the latest video game. They got Amish toys and trinkets. Presents were handed out to the children first. I had thought the gift-giving was over when Princess walked up to me with her hands behind her back and a devilish smile on her face. She took a minute and finally handed me the present she got for me. I unwrapped it to find a small wooden box, similar in size to an eyeglasses case. When I opened it, it had an old-school razor in it with a pack of blades. It was the kind of razor that you had to put the single edge blade into and tighten down with a screwdriver.

"Now, you can shave, dada." She said as she hugged me.

I thanked her. My beard had grown aggressively in the months since the war started. I had not given much thought to it. Hell, I always had one. However, during these hard times, if Princess wanted me to shave, I would. When everyone left, and before my shift began, I walked into the bathroom and shaved. I cut myself a few times, which didn't surprise me with that single edge blade. I could hear my wife getting the kids ready to go out back to see my Grandma, just as I walked out of the bathroom. Face smooth as a baby's ass. Princess stared at me for a moment.

"You look funny, dada." She said, giggling at me. Then She and handsome both hugged me as they walked out the door.

I suited up and made my way outside. Ann was waiting at the end of the driveway; she wanted to walk with me.

"Did you like your present from Princess?" she asked

"Of course, why wouldn't I?" I asked as she stopped in the road looking at me.

"I found a picture of you, in my things, from when we were together. You always had that clean, shaved look. Princess and I went for a walk the other day, and we stopped by my cabin. She saw the picture and asked who that was with me. When I told her it was he dada, she said that you looked so handsome and that you should shave off your beard. So I went up the hill and got that for her to give to you." She explained, standing shivering in the chill of the sun setting.

"I appreciate that you would do that for her; it means a lot to me. But I have to get to work; we can talk more again soon, ok?" I asked

Ann just smiled and walked off without saying another word.

I got to Alpha and started getting hell for losing the beard. Once I knew the team was squared away, I climbed into my hammock for some shuteye; it was going to be a hectic following day.

CHAPTER 9

I made sure the essential supplies were packed, an extra French press, my secret stash of Black Rifle coffee, and my desktop humidor. I mean, I was going to be out there a while, I wanted to make sure I enjoyed my time. I radioed up for someone to bring the tractor and trailer down to Main, so we could start loading everyone's gear on it. I then packed up extra equipment for the firing station as well, including several extra jerry cans for water, as well as all the MREs I had stashed in the basement. This was our first time using big green and a trailer to move supplies. Three-Three hopped on the tractor once it was loaded and headed up to Alpha to start unloading everything. Just then, I heard Ann's voice behind me.

"William, can we talk for a moment?" she asked.

"What can I do for you?" I asked as I turned around.

"I have been meaning to say thank you for saving my family and me from being killed. I am still so sorry for whatever I did to cause the fight between your wife and me". She said with a look in her eyes; I had not seen in a long time.

"If I had not been on my way home, you would have been on your own, so there is no need to thank me," I replied.

"I learned a lot from you when we were together, like having a plan, and the best plan I could come up with was to get to you because I knew that you would keep us safe," she continued to explain.

"Stop," I interrupted. "I do not want to hear it, nor do I need to. There is way more important shit going on around here than you and I or our past," I told her.

"I understand," she said with tears in her eyes as she stood up on her tiptoes, kissing me on the cheek before she walked away.

Her words tugged on my heartstrings a little, even when I have been trying to act tough as nails towards everyone because I believed that's what they needed to see from me, her words still got to me. Her words helped boost my confidence some, that all the decisions I had made up until this point had been the right ones. She always had that effect on me. Of course, I had not seen my wife at all until this very moment, and as expected, she came unglued.

"What the fuck did that stupid bitch kiss you for" she yelled as she walked towards me.

"Oh, my fuck, calm your ass down woman, all she did was thank me for saving her and her family's life," I told her.

"She fucking kissed you. I don't see why she needed to do that," still yelling.

"You know what, it was sweet, and honestly, it was a nice gesture during such a shitty time we are all living in, and since you have not been decent to anyone, including me since this shit started, it was needed," I told her.

"I am going to beat that stupid bitch" my wife started before I interrupted her.

"No, you're not. Maybe you could try being a whole lot more loving and understanding during these times. It would help. If you go after her again with your brand of stupid, I will send your ass packing. I don't care that you're the mother of my children at this point. They don't need your stupid, and neither does anyone else here. It was a kiss on the god damn cheek. It's not like she laid me on the ground and rode my dick, so grow the fuck up," I barked at her.

Once again, she walked away, unable to comprehend that it was nothing more than a thank you.

Three-Three finally arrived back with the tractor, after which he, Robin, and I made our way up to Alpha on foot. The weather had let up a little bit, so the hike up there wasn't so bad. Upon our arrival, Six-One and his team kept over-watch while we stowed our gear, and everyone set up their hammocks to sleep in.

When all of a sudden, Six-One started yelling, we had incoming traffic. I instantly ran to the bolt gun. Looking through the scope, I could see it was a late model truck with a plow being driven by a Hispanic adult male. The look on his face suggested he was more scared than he was looking for a fight.

Six-One ran towards the truck with his rifle pointed at the driver. The truck came to a stop about fifty yards from Alpha, and Six-One moved to the driver's side with his gun still pointed at the driver.

"Show me your hands," shouted Six-One.

The driver held up his left hand.

"Show me your fucking hands," shouted Six-One again.

"I did," shouted the driver.

"Show me your other fucking hand," shouted Six-One.

"I wish I could," shouted the driver.

"Show me your other fucking hand right now, or I will shoot you in the face," shouted Six-One as he moved just a little closer to the truck.

"I wish I could, but I can't," cried out the driver who was waving his left hand and his half missing right arm in panic.

I tried so hard not to, but I burst out laughing hysterically at the situation. Six-One's face instantly turned beat red as he heard not just me, but all of us laughing at him.

One-Three tapped me on the shoulder. "You're going to love this," he told me as he hit the push to talk button on his radio. "Two-Four this is One-Three, how copy?"

"I copy One-Three, what's up" replied Two-Four

"We have a Hispanic, military-age male up here at Alpha. We need a translator" One-Three said as he burst out laughing

"Seriously, what the fuck is wrong with you people, I've told you assholes before, just cause I'm brown doesn't fucking mean I speak Spanish," Two-Four was yelling into his radio.

We were all laughing, probably harder than we should have.

The man in the truck claimed he worked for a local farmer outside of our network zone. The farm he worked on was about four miles away. He had lost his right arm in a combine accident. He stepped out of the truck and was searched for weapons. He was wearing a yellow hoodie, jeans, and barn boots. The only thing we found on him was a lighter and a pack of cigarettes. He took off from the farm he worked at when the neighbors got attacked by a group of black or maybe Hispanic men. The only other information he could give us was that they were all approximately fighting-age males, there was eight perhaps ten of them, they had blue bandannas on their beltline, and they arrived in a Goldbeach city plow truck. At this time, our worst fears were coming true, their resources were used up, and they were looking for more. The driver told us he did not come to us looking for a fight. He was headed to Pennsylvania, where he had some family. We told him he could stay, but he was determined to get to his other family members. I understood that all too well.

He sat with us for a short bit; we gave him some food and water. The way he kept looking around was unsettling for me. Something was wrong; I could feel it. I walked out of earshot of the group and radioed to Main looking for descriptions of all the gangs we were able to get information about over the short-wave radio. While I was away from the group, he asked Six-One if it was ok that he got headed out; the sooner he got to his family, the better. I heard his truck start-up and started driving off as I got word back from Main; fifth on the list was a Hispanic gang who wore yellow shirts as one of the ways to identify themselves. I ran back to the group getting on the bolt gun, but as I turned to the direction he took off towards, he was already out of sight.

"FUCK" I yelled.

"What happened, boss," asked Robin.

"Congratulations, team, we just got tricked into taking in a possible forward observer for one of the biggest gangs in Goldbeach," I said.

At this time, I decided we needed to move the short-wave radio and all previous gathered intel to our station. This way, we would have all information necessary right there instead of having to ask for it.

I didn't sleep well that night. I kept hearing gunshots in the distance, they were not getting closer yet, but there wasn't a ton of obstructions between the farms where the shots were coming from and our location. It was not a matter of if they show up, because I could feel it in my bones that they were going to be on our doorstep at some point soon.

The morning came, and I brewed my very first cup of coffee for the day. The trainees were on the spotting scope, keeping watch as I lit a cigar to go with my coffee. We all were still making fun of Six-One, saying, "It wasn't me. It was the one-armed man". Fun and games aside, we had decided to keep all current team guys on shift at all times, with no training required for now. Trainees were still required to keep up with their training when it was my official time to be on watch; my trainees stayed as well as Six-One and Two-Eight, likewise when one of them was on shift, their trainees stayed with them.

My shift officially began as I threw my cigar; it was burning my fingers at that point; this also meant it was time for the other two groups of trainees to head off to their classes. Roughly thirty minutes into my shift, Two-Five radioed to me on the private channel that

Two-Eight's wife had suffered a nasty fall and hurt her arm bad; Doc and Two-Four were assessing her injuries. I told Six-One to escort Two-Eight back to Main as the news of this messed him up bad. The last thing we needed was for him to be in such a hurry to get back to Main that he hurt himself too. I told Six-One to radio when they were back at Main then to hurry his ass back once he got him to his wife.

I just got word they made it to Main; Six-One still had to get him to the town hall, then he would find out why the radio had not been moved yet, and be on his way back. Robin was on the spotting scope at that time, the weather seemed to have let up a bit more, and we had not heard gunshots in a few hours.

"Boss, I need you on the scope for a minute. I need you to confirm what I am seeing," Robin said with some panic in her voice.

I jumped on the bolt gun, swinging it to the west where Robin was already facing.

"Do you see that?" she asked.

There seemed to be a bright yellow, well something against a tree about eight hundred yards out. This was not normal; we had scoped every inch of the area from the firing station to one thousand yards out, there was nothing yellow on any trees. I kept my scope focused on that yellow patch just long enough to see half a face duck out from behind that tree. As he moved out from behind it ultimately to move to the next tree, I pulled the trigger to the rear on my rifle. It seemed like forever before the bullet impacted his chest, I was worried he would be able to get to his next point of cover before it did, but I saw him drop with a pink mist still in the air where he used to be standing. I instantly moved my scope to the other side of the road as I saw movement, there was another guy in a yellow hoodie moving towards us, again I fired, and again I hit. I yelled to Three-Three to get the belt-fed stationed next to me and to hold until they were within two hundred yards before he fired. I yelled for Robin to make her way to the tree line across from our position and hold fire unless someone got past Three-Three's line of fire. I could only hope at this moment that Six-One was hauling ass back.

Suddenly I saw movement centerline of the road; it was a city plow truck with a driver and one passenger inside. They were hauling ass towards our position. I lined my scope on the driver; I saw the round hit the windshield. I fired one more time at the driver before I saw him go limp. The passenger grabbed the wheel as he pushed his buddy out. I sent another shot it must have missed because that truck was now getting to close for comfort, one more round, and he went limp as well. The truck slowed down a lot before slipping off the road roughly three hundred yards away. The tailgate fell open, eight to ten men exited the rear armed with military-grade weapons, they opened fire on us. More men popped out of the tree line behind them, making their way closer to us. I continued to use the bolt gun, killing as many as I could before some got within range for Three-Three, he began shooting as fast as he could.

"Slowdown that damn gun, you're not hitting shit, make those fucking shots count god damn it," I yelled as I inserted another magazine into my rifle.

He slowed down alright and managed to hit three of them. They started to get smart, using the truck as cover, I grabbed my shotgun, telling Three-Three not to shoot me in the back as I ran out towards the truck. I got to the passenger side tire, dropping to my side, firing out the legs of three of them and finishing them off with shots to the face. I got up to a knee and began reloading my shotgun quickly. Two more guys fell at the hands of the belt-fed falling next to where I was kneeling. I popped out around the front of the truck when suddenly I felt an impact. I fell back, hitting the ground hard. I rolled towards the wheel well of the truck as fast as I could. One skinny ran around at me. I was able to get a shot off before he could. I went to pull the trigger again, but my shotgun seemed to quit working. I reached for my pistol just as another skinny came around the front. I felt two more impacts on my chest and a sudden burning sensation to my left arm. He pointed a handgun right at my face. It was our old friend, the one-armed man; just then, I saw his body start thrashing, blood pouring out of him, he fell to the ground. I looked back behind me to see Robin standing there, smoke coming out the end of the barrel on her rifle. She left a trail of bodies behind her as she moved towards the truck just in time to save my sorry ass.

Before I knew what was happening, Robin was on top of me applying a tourniquet to my left forearm. Stay here, don't move, she yelled at me as she pushed the button on my radio, calling for Two-Four and anyone else that could help.

"Get off me, woman, and help me up," I growled at her as I slapped her on the ass.

I got up to see Six-One covering us as we got back to the firing station.

It took Two-Four almost twenty minutes to get to me. "No worries, he said it was a threw and threw no bones broken, you will be fine, brother" as he looked at my arm. "Let's get you back to Main

Before I left, Robin cut and lit me a cigar; she figured why not it couldn't hurt. I puffed on it while I walked back with Two-Four. When I got to Main, Doc was waiting.

"Other than your arm have you been hit anywhere else?" asked Doc

"I took a few rounds to my hard plates, other than that I'm fine dad" I responded

"Don't fucking call me that in front of people," he said with a smile on his face as he packed my arm with gauze.

CHAPTER 10

I must have passed out. I woke on my dining room table with a large bandage on my left forearm. It hurt like hell. Doc was in my kitchen talking with both my wives; he was explaining that my wound was a through and through, through my left forearm with no bone breakage, and I would be okay with some reasonable time to heal. Both women were in tears, but they were supportive of each other. Maybe getting shot was a good thing to help settle all the crazy that had gone on. I walked into the kitchen; my chest was hurting as bad as my arm was because of the impact of three rounds to my plates. My wife and Ann both hugged me carefully; that was until I pointed out how well they were getting along and suggested a threesome, then my wife hit me.

Six-One was standing off to the side; he had radioed Two-Five that I was up and let him know what Doc had to say.

"Two-Five wants a word with you," as Six-One handed me the radio.

"Two-Five this is Six-Eight how copy?"

"Good copy, Six-Eight glad you are up. I need you at Alpha right now; we need to discuss this in person. How copy Six-Eight?"

"Good copy, Two-Five," I responded as I put on my battle belt, drawing my pistol assuring there was around in the chamber before I headed out. I walked to the back of the firing station to find Two-Five waiting for me.

"We again recovered documents from these assholes that had this location address on it. Also, a map with the layout of our firing stations and our total shooting team number of six men." He said aggressively

"Sounds to me like one of those that left were again possibly caught and tortured for information, FUCK!!" I shouted

"That's what I was thinking too. I'm guessing they came from the east because the forward observer noted that was the easiest way to come at us. With that group and the government issue weapons they had, they probably figured it would be an easy fight." he explained as he stood up.

"How many more people are going to come at us? Forty of them left here. We can guess at this point that two were captured." I explained as I looked around the station

"Let us worry about that for now, go be with your family and heal. I'm glad you're alive. Doc says it will take about a month before you can return to duty, so the team has voted you off duty till then, make the best of the days." said Two-Five.

"I want the radio moved from Main up to Alpha today. The delay in information cost us a gunfight we did not want or need at this time, and it can't happen again." I instructed Six-One as I left heading back to Main

"Wilco boss" he replied

My wife looked me in the eyes with a smile on her face as I returned, "Since you are off for the next month, it is bedtime, daddy," and led me up the stairs.

Both kids were upstairs waiting. My wife threw another log into the fireplace as my daughter jumped up and down on the bed, screaming, "yay daddy is coming to bed" as I laid down, she snuggled up to me instantly, not knowing yet to be careful because of my arm. My wife laid down on the bed, and my son laid on a mattress next to mommy's side of the bed. I shut off the oil lamp and closed my eyes.

My eyes opened at 0600. It felt like the last few months had been a terrible dream until the pain in my chest and arm decided to remind me otherwise. I got dressed, making my way downstairs, where I was mobbed by two overly excited children, and my wife greeted me with a cup of coffee. I sat at the table listening to my children chatter away about all the things they had been doing while daddy was working, just then it hit me what the real cost of this war was ultimately going to be on us all.

When I was done with my coffee, I got up from the table and told my wife to get our son ready for some outdoor time with daddy. I went to the basement and retrieved our snowshoes, went back upstairs, and when he was ready, we started on our journey. We left Main and headed up the trail, passing by the pavilion headed into the woods. It took a while with his little feet not able to carry him as fast as I could move, but we went at his pace. We arrived at the Bravo firing station; Six-Six had a small fire going where we boiled some water for a hot chocolate break, well for him anyway, I brewed another cup of coffee. We sat and talked with the uncles for a short while, then made our way down the trail towards Alpha. We stopped there for a bit; I explained to my son what we did there before we headed back to Main.

Once we returned, I bundled up the princess, and all three of us began playing in the snow in the front yard. Richard walked out front asking if he and his children could join us; I told him, of course, they could.

We had a family against family snowball fight; afterward, we built a snowman army. The army consisted of fifteen snowmen. As cold as we all were, we decided to make a snow angel field. Each of us made three snow angels covering the rest of the yard behind our snowmen. We all agreed to go inside after that; Ann was in the kitchen with Robert. I asked her to make a round of hot chocolate for the minions. Once we all got our snow gear off, the coco was served to us at the dining room table. Once we were done, we all headed out back for dinner.

After all the fun we had, I sat with my children and read to them. Unfortunately, my library was not geared towards children, but I don't think they cared very much. It took me nearly three hours to read the first half of American Sniper to them; I am relatively sure I had been reading to two snoring children for the last half-hour; we would finish the rest the next day. My wife carried up Handsome, and I carried up Princess. It was roughly 2 am when I was awoken by Princess, kissing me and telling me she loves me; she rolled right back over and went back to sleep.

The next morning, I woke before my family did. I made my way downstairs to the kitchen and brewed a cup of coffee. Drinking my coffee, I planned out my day with the kids. Once they were done with classes, I took Handsome to the basement, got out his BB gun, and set up a target. The deal was he got ten BBs. For every point he got on the bullseye target, he got that many more BBs to shoot. This was my way of teaching him the value of each shot. The better he shot, the more chances he would get. We spent a lot of time in the basement. He got six "x" ring shots, two 8's and two 7's. Even earning all those extra shots, he still had to take his time and try to get then in a tight shot group.

We finished and made our way upstairs. I found Princess, and we played her favorite game, the beat on daddy relentlessly game. She would stand on my stomach while I laid on my back, holding both of my hands swinging back and forth, then BOOM! She would kick her legs out from underneath herself and drop all her thirty-eight pounds down on my stomach. Then she wanted to run circles around me. At the same time, I laid on my stomach, trying to catch or trip her; if I got her, I would drag her to me and tickle her senseless. This meant I got to listen to the most adorable laughter and snorting, probably my most favorite sound in the world. We went to dinner. Then we finished the other half of our book before bed.

Morning came; life almost seemed normal again. After classes, we went back to a long day of shenanigans. Once bedtime came, I was tired, but my mind was racing, thinking about the team, what could happen next, how could we deal with it, when suddenly, like the night before, my daughter rolled over kissing me, " I love you dada" she said in the cutest sleepy voice on earth. It was almost as if she could sense my anxiety and woke just to settle me if that was the case; it worked. "I love you to Princess," I said to her and fell asleep almost instantly with a smile on my face. I woke feeling more refreshed than I had this entire time off duty. The day went as usual coffee, then waiting for the kids to be home.

Things were different when the kids came home on this day; however, my son was being extremely whiney and had an uncompromising attitude. When I asked my son what was wrong, he started crying. Princess took my hand, looked up at me, and said, "I'm being good dada." I asked her what his problem was. She shrugged her shoulders, turned to him, and said, "No, screaming and crying" as much as I tried not to, I could not help but laugh a little, which of course made his screaming and crying get worse.

"Come on, Handsome, enough with that shit," I said to him. Suddenly Princess said "My daddy said enough"

"Princess," I said as I looked at her, "You let daddy do daddy things, ok."

"Why don't you go sit on the couch," I said as I turned to my son, "until you get your shit together, then we can all have fun."

Of course, this made it worse, and he got even louder. "What the fuck did you do?" my wife asked as she walked into the room

Before I could get a word out "my daddy told him to stop screaming and crying" Princess pipped up

"Princess, let mommy and daddy talk, ok." I told her as I turned towards my wife, "I didn't do shit to him, he walked in from school whining like a two-year-old, had he walked in like the almost six-year-old he is, there would not be any issues."

In her typical fashion, my wife replied "whatever" and walked out of the room, with my son following behind her looking for coddling.

I decided to make my way to the cave for a bit, like usual, Princess followed behind me. Just as we got downstairs, my wife yelled down that my grandfather was upstairs looking for me. He came down and sat chatting with Princess and me while she and I played a game of chess; she played a mean game too. After about an hour of conversation and games, we all went back upstairs. Handsome seemed to be in a way better mood; we went to dinner than back home for some reading.

The night came as did bedtime. It was around two am when Princess woke screaming and terrified because bugs were crawling on her. When I looked, there was nothing. She kept swatting and screaming at the bugs. It took forty-five minutes for my wife and I to calm her down, pulled the blanket over her, and she started to fall back to sleep when fifteen minutes later, she was screaming again. She threw her blanket on the floor. She said the bugs were on her blanket. It took another thirty minutes of explaining and showing her there were no bugs, but damn she did not believe us. I realized there would be no convincing her, so I showed her there were no bugs on my blanket. After about five minutes, she finally agreed there was not. She then crawled under my blanket with me, insisting that I hold her to keep her safe. She eventually fell back to sleep. I woke in the morning with her still wrapped up in my arms; she was smiling a little bit as she snored.

As the kids were at school that day, I worked on a big surprise for them. I found my old laptop down in the cave and plugged it into the solar charger, hoping it would hold a charge. Just before they got done with school, I took it off the charger and picked a movie for us to watch. I told them if they were extra good tonight, I had a surprise for them. Dinner was over, and they were begging for their surprise. I told them to sit on the couch, set the laptop on the coffee table. When they saw the DVD box in my hand, they got so excited. They fell asleep in my arms halfway through watching Captain America.

The weeks had gone by way to fast. Doc was in my kitchen when I walked down for my morning coffee. He was there to give me the go no go for duty. My grandpa was with him, waiting to see the same as myself if I was cleared to go back to work. Doc gave me the all-clear, my plan at this point was to make a full week of training before heading back into the field. I decided to make my way to the cave while the kids were at school. Grandpa followed me down with a plastic bag in hand.

I grabbed a Perdomo Small Batch from my humidor, cut, and lit it. My grandpa and I sat talking; well, he spoke as I listened. He told me how scared he was when he heard I had been shot, how he wished this hell had never happened, but how proud of me he and my grandma were. He talked about his trips to Africa and Cuba, how I would have loved going to the cigar factories. He got up to leave; I gave him a huge hug telling him how much I loved him and grandma. He pulled a stuffed rabbit from the plastic bag. He said to me that I had forgotten it at his house some thirty years earlier. I teared up some, I did not remember ever having it, but he sure did. He had been meaning to give it to me all these years but had kept forgetting. Had I known this would be the last time we ever spoke, I may have said more.

He left the cave that day; my uncle was supposed to walk him back to the cabin where he and grandma stayed, but apparently, he did not. We had a more substantial snowfall; on his way back alone, he fell off the side of the trail down a short hill, hitting his head on a tree stump. It was two days before he was found. The weather had let up, the snow melted slightly, which uncovered his body. Doc said, based on the head trauma, he most likely died instantly with no suffering; it certainly did not make me feel better about the situation.

My brother and I made him a casket; Doc recommended that we cremate him due to the frozen ground and weather conditions. This would later become our standard care for our dead. We had a service for him; everyone not on duty attended. The hardest part of this for me was explaining to my children that their great-grandpa was no longer with us; Princess said she wanted to kiss him. I broke down crying.

CHAPTER 11

After the funeral services for my grandfather, I returned to Main with my wife and kids. I told my wife I needed some time to myself and made my way down to the cave. I found One-Three sitting at a table with two glasses and a bottle of Lead Slinger's bourbon like he had been waiting for me. I grabbed, cut, and lit a cigar as I turned towards him.

"Have a seat," said One-Three as he poured our first glass

I walked to the table and sat down. "What's on your mind, brother," I asked as I took my glass and raised it to his company.

"Brother, I know you got a lot going on," he said as he raised his glass to me with a look of concern on his face, "But I thought you should be aware, Two-Five wants to have a vote to remove you from the team permanently."

I sipped my bourbon, feeling the burn as it went down to my stomach, "Does he feel this is what is best for the team?" I asked.

"He feels the recent loss of your grandpa will take away from your mission focus, the constant chaos between your wife and your ex he feels has caused laps in focus, and he does not believe you can come back from the fact you got shot," said One-Three.

"What are your thoughts, brother?" I asked.

"I think," he took a sip from his glass, "I think you have already bounced back from being shot. Any of the problems that have been between your wives you have dealt with mostly off duty. Though some have been on duty, that is no different than dealing with Carl's bullshit on duty. I say you take a week or two, hit all the training classes you can, test and prove Two-Five wrong," he said.

"That is not what I asked you, brother" I paused to look at my cigar "what do you think?"

"I think Two-Five is still pissed because you called a vote against him, and we all voted in favor of what is best for the team. I think we could handle this whole mess without you, let you be with your children, and just take an instructor role. However, there are not many people on this earth besides you that I would want fighting next to me, and I don't believe there is anyone better to run the unit," he explained.

We sat in silence for the remainder of our drink, One-Three left before I was finished with my cigar. I got in some serious playtime with the kids before bed, the plans I had for myself would keep me busy for the next two weeks.

Morning came; after my coffee, I made my way out back to our training sight. Richard was delighted to see me there. I partnered up with Two-Eight. I started slowly, and as the hours passed, I could feel the hurt, but I had no interest in stopping now. I took the short break in between hand-to-hand class and the weapons training class, then the next break before more hand-to-hand training with Richard and Robin. Doubling up on classes was not the brightest idea I had, but it was the best idea if I was going to prove my worth to the team. I needed a triumphant return. I needed it for myself, not just the team. Another break and back to weapons training. When bedtime came, my ass was out cold quickly.

I continued my double training days for two weeks straight, partnering with Two-Eight for every class he was there for. When the two weeks were over, I instructed Richard to test me. It had to be a higher standard of grading than ever before. I wanted my test results to be given to Six-One and Two-Five only.

When testing was over, I went back to Main, got dressed, grabbed my guns and gear, and headed off to Alpha. It was nice to be back up there, especially since that's where my stash of Black Rifle coffee was hidden. I started brewing a pot instantly. As I waited for the water to boil, I walked across the tent to our new radio station and map center when I could not believe my eyes.

"What in the unholy fuck is that?" I asked.

"What?" said One-Three.

"Don't fucking look at me," said Six-One "It was his idea."

"What are my son's toy cars and army men doing on the map?" I asked.

"Neither of your kids play with them anymore," said One-Three.

"Seriously, what's wrong with using post-it notes?" I asked

"In a time of limited supply, we should remember post-it notes are not reusable, and besides now the map looks like the ones the generals used in the world war two movies," said One-Three with a very creepy level of excitement in his voice

"You have got to be kidding me," I said as I put my hands over my face, "you are like a fucking little kid."

One-Three was awfully proud of the decision he had made. I walked back to my pot and put the coffee in the press when Six-One went over the radio. "I just received word from our training division, Six-Eight has passed all of the testing well within the new required standards outlined for him to return to duty."

"When I call your name, give a yes or no vote" Two-Five came over the radio.

He called each team member by callsign over the radio with everyone voting yes, much to his disappointment, I was sure.

"The majority has voted, Six-Eight has retaken command of Alpha team," Said Six-One over the radio.

Six-One handed me a radio. "This is Six-Eight, I am officially back on duty. The first order of business is the physical testing results for Two-Five; he passed. Congratulations, you will remain on duty," I said.

Now that those matters were put to rest, we could move forward. I asked Two-Five, Two-Eight, and Six-Six to meet me in the cave to discuss an idea I had in my downtime. I was first down there, per usual, I grabbed myself a much-deserved cigar. Once the others arrived, we got down to business.

"Two-Eight and Six-Six I need to know right now, no bullshit, how are your trainees doing?" I asked.

They both looked at me and, in unison, said they were doing well.

"Are you both willing to bet your life on them, yes or no?" I asked.

"yes boss," replied Two-Eight

"yes," said Six-Six

"Since you both feel that way, I am giving you your own team. You guys will take your trainees and move your gear to the farm. In the event we are attacked the way we were before, the farm was left open for attack, and I do not wish for that to happen again. Alpha will provide overwatch of the farm in the event of an attack from that direction. Two-Eight you have the most experience between the two of you, so you will be the one in command, Six-Six you will be his second. Either of you have a problem with this?"

"No boss," said Two-Eight

"Nope," said Six-Six

"Do either of you have any questions?" I asked

"What is going on with our wives?" asked Six-Six

"This will be a permanent move, so tell them to pack their things as they are going with you," I said.

"Wilco boss" replied Six-Six

"Any more questions?" I asked

"No" they both replied

"Good go pack your things, tell your team they go live tomorrow, get your guard rotation figured out by then, and get out of my sight," I told them

They turned and left the cave. Two-Five turned to go as well.

"Hold up Two-Five," I said

"What the fuck do you want now?" he asked

"Tell One-Three he has command for the next twenty-four hours, and you meet me at the training sight in thirty minutes," I said.

"What the fuck for?" he asked with a growl in his voice

"In the next twenty-four hours, you and I are either going to put this bullshit to rest, or we are going to kill each other," I said.

"I can't fucking wait," he said as he walked out of the room.

I took off my duty gear, grabbed my boxing gloves, making my way out back to the pavilion. I met up with Richard and told him what had been going on while I awaited Two-Fives arrival.

"How do you want to do this?" asked Richard.

"Full five-minute rounds with thirty-second breaks in between, until one of us is knocked out or cannot possibly fight any longer." I told him as I grabbed my radio, "One-Three I need you to put a bottle and two glasses on the bar, I am not sure how long this will last; however, the cave will be our next stop."

"Wilco boss," said One-Three.

Two-Five came walking up, he stripped off his gear and strapped on his boxing gloves. Richard explained to him how the rounds would go. We walked to the center of the pavilion, touched gloves, then went back to opposite sides when Richard yelled, "GO," we met again in the middle. We moved around for a few moments before Two-Five started throwing punches. I planned to cover and block as much as I could while Two-Five got his frustration out. His technique was pretty good, and near the end of the first round, I screwed up. I felt my head snap back, and to the right, as Two-Five landed a solid hit, my eye was going to swell up from that one.

Round two was the same tactics on my part. Though I covered better this time to avoid being hit again in the face, it certainly cost me several shots to the body. The round ended, but Two-Five was still swinging away. Richard stepped in and broke us up. Two-Five was muttering to himself as he walked to his corner about the fact I was not fighting back.

Round three and four were the same. I took several shots to the body and, unfortunately, several more to the left side of my face. I could tell at the end of the fourth Two-Five was getting beyond tired. His arms looked like they were heavy for him as he was even more frustrated that I continued not to fight back.

"Why the fuck are you not fighting back, fucking fightback already" he screamed at me.

He asked for a fight; a fight is what I gave him. The fifth round began, both of us meeting in the middle. I continued to block and cover, waiting for the right moment as his technique began to fall short of an angry child. Three minutes into the round, I found my opening. His head snapped back as I caught him with a beautiful uppercut followed by a right cross, his head snapping to the right. I threw a double jab to his face right after causing him to cover his face exposing his core to me. I went to work hammering on his core. He tried to cover his body as he started to lose his balance, that's when I knocked him to the ground with another right cross.

He hit the ground hard. I instantly took off my right glove extending out my hand to help him to his feet. He was a bit disorientated. Richard instructed both of us to sit for a short while and put some snow on our faces. We sat in silence for a good thirty minutes; when I stood up to leave, I looked at Two-Five.

"Grab your gear and meet me in the cave in twenty minutes," I said.

Two-Five nodded. I walked down to Main, took a few minutes to wash up before heading down to the cave. I poured bourbon into the glasses that One-Three had set out for us, placed them on the table before getting myself a cigar. I grabbed Two-Five's favorite pipe off the shelf, got him some tobacco, and laid it with his glass. Two-Five finally made his way downstairs, taking a seat in front of his pipe and drink.

"How is your face besides still ugly as fuck?" he asked as he struck a match to light his pipe.

I looked up from lighting my cigar "better than yours fuck face, hence why I am married, and you are not," I said.

"That don't mean shit, even a blind squirrel gets a nut every once in a while," he said, pausing to exhale "besides, your wife doesn't even like you."

"There is definitely truth to that statement," I said, "however she seems to like me more than my second in command does lately, you going to tell me what the fuck the problem is, brother?"

"I brought that up for a vote because I thought it was in the best interest of the team. The team obviously felt otherwise," he said.

"You want to know what I am thinking?" I asked, "I'm thinking that you are still pissed over the vote I called for, that you took that shit personally, instead of looking at it from the perspective of what is best for the team. Would you seriously want extra fat fuck Robbie running a gun next to you when he could not run ten feet before without nearly having a fucking heart attack"?

"No," he said, "I just thought."

"You didn't think," I interrupted him, "you called for your vote out of anger and spite. You fought me out back out of anger and look where that got you, you fucking lost." I sipped from my glass.

"You're right," he said. "I would never let forty pounds ago Robbie fight alongside me, fuck I am not even one hundred percent sure of him now. Just tell me something; why did you wait till the fifth round to fight back?"

"Why fight you when your anger was fighting against you?" I said, "Anger was and is your worst enemy at a time like this, I could have probably knocked you out early, but you needed to get the anger out, to see what your anger was causing and ultimately cost you in that fight. I did not fight you out of anger. I fought you to get your anger out," I told him.

"You have to admit, your wife and ex-wife have caused you a lot of grief, and that can distract you from the mission, brother," said Two-Five.

"Even with as often as you were at the house, I often forget that you're not married, brother. All the married team guys have gone through similar moments with their wives. The only difference is that you have been witness to most of it because those crazy bitches make it a scene for everyone, with emphasis on my current wife. All the team guys have had problems with their wives since this shit started, they talk to me and each other about it because we are all married, and we can relate to each other's problems where you can't, and if you took some of your downtimes, as I always do, to spend with my kids you would understand that I am nowhere near distracted from our mission, they are the mission brother" I said

"Wilco boss, another glass?" he said.

"Yeah, why the fuck not? We have other business to discuss anyway," I said.

He poured us both another glass.

"We got hit pretty hard, but we also got very god damn lucky, would you agree?" I asked.

Two-Five nodded as he re-lit his pipe.

"What I am thinking is a two-man recon team, we go out with the bolt gun and spotting scope, we run surveillance sending all the intel in real-time back to the radio station at Alpha so they can put on the map what is where to help update our previously gathered intel. The attackers came from Goldbeach, but Goldbeach will have to wait.

I want to know what we missed locally that slipped those fuckers in from the back door," I told him.

"Makes sense to me" replied Two-Five

CHAPTER 12

In truth, Two-Five and One-Three were far better precision rifle shooters than I was. However, Two-Five and I agreed that it would hurt the teams if two guys off one team went. It would be Two-Five and I going. For this mission, Two-Five would be operating the bolt gun relaying information back to Alpha. At the same time, I ran security for him and spent time on the spotting scope, communicating what information I could as well. The idea was to use our radios as if we were talking to each other, while Alpha listened in and made all the appropriate intel updates on the map.

All original team members were made aware of what we were doing. However, they were not to share that information with anyone, not their families, trainees, and especially not my family. We did not want anyone to worry or panic over us not being around.

We gathered our gear; I packed Betty, enough shell cards for my QDC to resupply my chest rig and battle belt three times and fifteen extra pistol mags. The mission called for five days as we planned it. So naturally, I packed two change of socks and underwear per day, one MRE per day, two extra radio batteries, additional personally needed items, also carried extra magazines for the bolt gun. I told my wife and kids I would be staying at Alpha for the next few days; if we saw any attacks again, it would be best to have all hands on deck as before. As per the usual, my wife walked away, muttering what I like to call "suggestive insults."

Due to the still very frigid temperatures in February, we decided it best to start at first light, just as the sun was coming up, and all team leaders were on duty. We strapped on our snowshoes and moved to the east of Alpha. It was a six-mile hike, in pretty bad weather, to our first recon position. We stuck to the same pattern of movement I used to get home from Goldbeach.

Two miles into our journey, we came to a field owned by a farmer named Mark. I knew him vaguely before the war started; we used to buy hay from him and his son. As protocol had it, we made our way one hundred yards to the east of the top of his field, and then we heard shots being fired. It seemed the shot could have come from the house on the other side of the field, possibly being fired in our direction. We heard another shot; there was no bullet splash in the snow around us, or anywhere near us for that matter. I took out the spotting scope to see what I could.

"What do you see, brother," asked Two-Five.

"I can see his house, approximately eight hundred fifty yards out," I said just as a third shot rang out.

Two-Five unpacked the tripod for the bolt gun and set up.

"He is in the top left bedroom window of his house. He is shooting into the field below, not at us." I said.

"Fuck!" he said as he looked over the field.

"What," I asked.

"Look in the field, thirty-three posts across, eighteen down," he said.

I quickly followed his directions. I saw two people lying dead on the ground; they were unarmed; they must have been trying to cross the open field in search of safety. When I noticed movement in the top corner of my scope, so I adjusted to see better. There sat an abandoned red tractor with a yellow country line seed spreader mounted on it. On the side of the spreader, crouched down, was a woman holding her child, breathing heavily, looking back at the dead crying, terrified and unarmed. Suddenly a fourth shot broke, the bullet punched through the bright yellow plastic passing through the other side, exiting through the woman's chest into her child's head. Both of their bodies fell to the ground. Two-Five witnessed the same as I had.

"Range that mother fucker NOW," he said.

"My best guess is still eight hundred fifty yards, looks to be a fifteen mile per hour wind coming in from the north," I told him.

I watched the rifle shift slightly, he worked the action and sent one round towards the house, then worked the action again.

"I do not see any movement in the window; it was a good shot, brother," I said.

He held his scope on the window for a minute after, as did I, then someone appeared and fired a shot in our direction. The bullet hit a medium-size tree, nearly cutting it in half, almost thirty yards in front of us.

"I think he switched to a 50 Cal," said Two-Five.

When a second bullet hit not far from the same spot, Two-Five fired again, we both held scope on the window for the next five minutes with no more movement to be seen and no more shots fired.

"We can clear his house to be sure on our way back," I said.

It was near nightfall when we hit our first recon position. It was a mid-point on dead man's hill, probably the steepest hill in our area. I forget what the real name of the road was. At the top of the hill was an overlook. Come summer, people would drive from all over to come to it. You could see the entire town below. Of course, the whole town below could see people at the overlook if they wanted too.

We set up our overwatch position in the woods just below the overlook, the trees there would provide us cover, and we could still see the town below. We set up camp for the night taking four-hour shifts on watch while the other slept. Two-Five was still really amped up from what happened at Mark's farm, not to say that it was not affecting me as well; he just seemed to be taking it a bit harder. Once the fire was going, we put up a tarp on the town side of our fire to keep the light as dim as possible, in case someone below was watching above for onlookers such as us. We both filled out our field notes on what had occurred earlier; once I was done, I climbed my ass into my hammock and tried to sleep. Unfortunately, as life would have it, every time I closed my eyes, all I could see was the fear on that woman and child's faces. I spent most of my time wondering if we could have reacted faster or if we were, in fact, too late to help when we got there. I got maybe thirty minutes of uninterrupted sleep; it could not have been much more than that honestly. I got up and made my way over to the fire; we did not say much to one another as Two-Five got up and went over to the hammock to try and rest himself. I could hear him struggling, I imagine much like I did, to get sleep. Trying to keep the fire small, I had to sit closer to it to get the chill out of my body.

The hours had passed, and it was near time to wake Two-Five, so I got out my coffee stash and started melting snow, getting it to a boil before I woke him. He climbed out of the hammock grunting, and in an overall bad mood, it was apparent he slept as good and as much as I did.

"Want some coffee to help brighten your day thunder cloud?" I asked.

"Is that your super-secret stash of Black Rifle coffee?" he asked with a chuckle.

"Fuck, yes, it is," I said.

"Well, fuck yes, I do, bout god damn time you let me dip into that," he said.

We sat sipping our coffee as we waited for the sun to come up over the hill. It would be above us before it covered the town, but it would give us time to make sure we were set up with proper over-watch positioning. We could see some lights moving around the town below, but until the sun was up, it was hard to tell for sure what we were looking at.

The sun was finally blanketing the town, and our mission was about to begin. We first had to verify that Alpha would be able to hear our radio transmission.

"This is Two-Five come in radio."

"Two-Five, this is Six-One, we hear you loud and clear over."

"Copy that radio," said Two-Five.

"Two-Five, stop calling me radio over."

"Ok, radio."

"You done Two-Five?"

"Yes, radio."

I about fell over laughing; what made it even funnier was that for a guy who wanted to be a cop, Six-One had never seen Super Troopers until like a week before the war started. It was a much-needed shot of humor after the day we had previously. From our position, we could see the south side of the town center pretty well. We began transmitting what we saw over the radio.

"I have movement, North West building from center, second floor."

"Copy, I see it, it looks like someone is just peeking out."

"The old hotel on the southwest corner of center has a big red X on the back, looks like some ass-hat spray-painted it on."

"Copy, hold one, I got a runner, coming from the old repair shop southeast corner of center, looks like he is headed towards the apartment on the northwest corner."

"Probably what the peeker was looking for, I have two military-age males exiting the back of the hotel, one black one white; they seem to be arguing."

"Copy, I see them."

"They are both armed. They appear to have a matching red X on their jackets. The black dude seems he could give a fuck what slim shady has to say."

"A second black male is exiting the back of the hotel headed towards your boys."

"Copy, he is coming into my crosshairs, HOLY SHIT he just shot slim shady in the back of the head."

"Got a half-naked black female exiting the back of the hotel."

"Got her, she seems to be pleading with the guy that just shot shady, FUCK, first dude just walked up and shot her in the face."

"Makes you wonder what twisted love triangle bullshit just happened."

"Shit is better than cable. I know that."

"The two men have wandered back into the hotel."

"got a peeker in the top window of the hotel too."

"I see them."

All that happened before 10 am, the rest of our day was eerily quiet, with only seeing two more people and one car making its way through the town center. As the hours past, we discussed our plans for movement to the east side of town. The best vantage point was what was now an abandoned gas station. This would, however, put us within four hundred fifty yards of center, which also meant we would not be able to camp like we had the night before.

We packed up our gear as the sun was beginning to set. We had to use what sunlight we could to help us navigate the woods to town but needed the darkness once we got close to conceal our movement. It took almost two hours to get through the woods to the outskirts of town. There were a lot of houses, so we had to be extra careful with our movement. Hopefully, none of those houses had lookouts that could give away our position. Most of the homes we passed had their windows boarded up, and some had lookout holes cut into them; almost all of them had some type of bullet holes in them too. Some of the houses, we could see a glow behind the covered windows, like some poor soul still lived in them.

We came across one house, covered in bullet holes like the others, with two bodies halfway hanging out from two separate windows like they had made a stand against whatever evil came their way, but they did not fall. Judging by the number of bullet holes in the side of the house, the poor bastards never stood a chance.

Finally, we made it to the gas station; we cleared it well for a couple of jackasses that never received SWAT training. We took an old office inside as our rest location. We did our predetermined four-hour watch and rest rotation, turning on a small camp stove, every two hours, in the office to try and take the chill out of the air to help us rest.

I took first watch this time, keeping myself back from the big windows, I positioned myself behind some old shelving so I could see through all the windows without being seen. Looking around at what was nothing but trash left after the station had probably been looted, I noticed several empty two-liter soda bottles. I remembered a movie I had watched as a child, where the hero taped a soda bottle to the end of his pistol as a poor man's suppressor. I decided to go to the office and retrieve a roll of electrical tape from my bag; as I walked in, I could hear Two-Five faintly snoring. I walked back to the shelving and proceeded to tape a soda bottle to the end of my pistol. In the event of an enemy encounter, I could only hope it would work.

Two hours into my shift, I saw a pair of flashlights approaching the station. Once they got closer, I could see it was two male skinnies with a red X on their jackets and a female. They came inside, proceeded to get undressed, and had a very intense threesome. I looked over to see Two-Five peeking through the door with his pistol ready in case things turned to hell quick. Thirty minutes later, they had finally finished up. As they dressed, they became startled by a noise I heard not far from me. It sounded like it was actually above me. They started shining their lights all over and pointing their weapons in my general direction. Just then, a stray cat fell from the ceiling tile. They laughed it off while picking up empty soda bottles and throwing them at the poor cat. They finished getting dressed and exited our location, making their way to the old hotel.

Two-Five managed to get another hour of sleep after his heart rate went back to normal. He woke up, and I explained my soda bottle suppressor idea to him. He proceeded to tape a bottle to his pistol. I got lucky; I got a full four hours of sleep. I awoke to a pot of freshly brewed coffee, and we began setting up the watch nest for the day. The sun was up; it was time to go to work.

"I got two skinnies on the upper-level deck of the hotel and two on the lower level deck, all appear armed."

"Copy, I see our peeker in the apartment building second-floor window again."

"You think maybe they are gathering intel like we are?"

"It is a possibility."

"Looks to be a possible guard shift change, both first and second floor, it is 0900, set of two guards is being replaced by a set of two, also armed."

"Copy. I noticed they didn't have any guards on the south side of the building."

"Makes for an obvious entry point if we have to."

"Agreed."

"I got a military issue, Humvee, traveling from the west, headed towards center, it appears to have a Nazi flag on the grill."

"Shit is about to get real fucking serious, really fucking fast."

"No, shit, right."

The truck stopped in front of the hotel; four well-armed whites got out of the truck, one stood there waving a second Nazi flag, all appeared to be taunting the Red X gang members. The Red X guys on guard were pointing their guns at the Nazis, and both groups were shouting at each other, but no one seemed dare pull the trigger.

"I have a third guy exiting a door on the second floor of the hotel, he appears unarmed, joining the guards."

"I got him; I think that is the same guy that shot the half-naked woman yesterday."

"I do believe so."

"I think that he may be the man in charge."

"Agreed."

The four Nazi scumbags got back into their truck and turned down the street headed north away from center. It was about four hours before the truck had returned, again the shouting and pointing of weapons occurred till the Red X boss came out and shut that down again. The truck made the same turn again north away from center.

As darkness fell, we began packing our gear to move. The plan at this time was to make our way north of center. There was a state shock prison located there, maybe a mile down the road. Early reports had indicated that the prisoners had managed to escape and burn the prison to the ground; I hoped that one of the watchtowers would still be standing. I knew a guy who worked there before the war, he told me from that tower, with excellent glass, you could see all the way to center.

CHAPTER 13

We were deep in town, so we had no choice but to wait for total darkness before we could move. When it came time, our movement was slow, the clouds covered the moon, and we could not use our lights for fear of giving away our presence to any possible lookout. It took a little over an hour to get to the outskirts of town. We dug some red cellophane from our bags, wrapping it over the lenses of our lights, taping it in place, and used our low light training to get our asses out of town.

It took us about two hours from there to get to the south side of the prison. Our dreams of being able to build a nice fire and keep out of the wind were shot down upon our arrival. It appeared a large group of people was occupying the prison. We decided we would make our way up the east side wall past the prison to see what we could find for shelter; we hit the far east corner and found nothing. We moved north another half mile and found an abandoned house; we took shelter there. It took us a little while to find enough stock to keep a fire going throughout the night. Once the fire was going, Two-Five took the first rest as I stood watch.

I sat watching the stars through a window, thinking about my kids, hoping there was an end to this war before they would have to fight at my side. It was the first time in a long time I thought about something other than keeping the team going in the right direction. I woke Two-Five after four hours and took some rest. I must have fallen asleep fast; I don't remember much after my head hit the pillow. Two-Five woke me with a fresh cup of brew. We sat sipping away slowly; when done, we packed and prepared to move.

We chose to make our way to the west side of the prison. That's was where the main entrance was. It was a heavily wooded area with a severely fire damaged house about fifty yards away. We set our position. The first thing we saw was some of the parking lot lights were on, then hanging between three windows in the third story was a massive Nazi flag it draped down to the first floor. In the front was a small snow-covered mound. Four bodies were lying on top, all dark skin, all in prison jumpsuits.

"I am beginning to think the early reports of this place burning up were a bit off; it looks like the crazy whites found a place to call home," said Two-Five.

The sun came up enough to shed light on things we could not see outside of the few parking lot lights that were on. We began radio transmissions.

"I see three gas tankers parked along the wall, south side of the parking lot."

"Explains how they have lights on, hijacked them to keep the generators going."

"Makes sense to me, I see six small trucks similar in size to the one they were using to taunt the Red X boys, makes sense now why they didn't take that fight."

"Would have been fun to watch though, I'm seeing what looks like a six-man guard rotation happening on the southeast corner."

"Copy, I see what looks like maybe thirty heavily armed males exiting the front, armed with what looks like M4 rifles, maybe some Ak's."

Just then, my finger slipped off my push to talk button on my radio. "FUCK ME; they have a radio tower we need to move NOW!!!"

Two-Five sprang up to a knee, shouldering his rifle and flipping off the safety "Break squelch twice when you have me covered, I'll cover you until then."

At this moment, if we moved to fast, we would be seen if we moved to slow, we would be caught. I got fifty yards past our position, posted myself behind a tree, broke squelch, dropped my safety, and provided cover. Two-Five got fifty yards behind me and did the same. We repeated this leapfrog process until we hit a creek bed, probably two hundred yards beyond where we started. There was enough snow on the ground unless the crazy whites were completely stupid, they could follow us out, so the decision to take to the creek was easy. This would undoubtedly mean wet feet, but that beat being dead hands down.

We trudged through the water quickly. We could still hear the crazy whites behind us, they were, however, out of sight, and their sounds were getting more faint with every step. We cut back into the woods about a mile up from where we went into the creek and ducked into the woods about one hundred yards. We sat trying to catch our breath as Two-Five said, "Well, I guess we're done at this location."

"No, we're not, we have to go back, I will swear on my life just before I picked up the scope to move, I saw Mustang Sally," I said.

"Are you fucking kidding me? What would that ass clown be doing with them? He's a total fucking asshole but, I have never known him to be a racist asshole," said Two-Five.

Mustang Sally was a guy we both knew from years back. He worked for my family for several years, older than me with fifteen years in the national guard, never making it past the rank of specialist, we figured because of his mouth. Bought himself one of the new "old body style" mustangs when they first came out. He couldn't afford the big engine, so he bought the small one and put stickers all over it, making people think it had the big engine in it. He was not someone you could trust in a situation like we were in, but Two-Five was right; he was not a racist, that was why I needed to be sure if it was or was not him.

"If it was, in fact, Sally, he was probably on his way to PA or our area when he was caught and is now playing Nazi to save his own scumbag ass," I said.

"So, what the fuck are we going to do now then," asked Two-Five.

"We have to pick a new spot for recon. Unfortunately, the best spot now will be that fire-damaged house. It will still give us a good line of sight, and the fuckers will never look for us in a location we were already in, and we are going to have to stay off our radios." I told him.

I hit the push to talk button on my radio, "Melody Green." I say again, "Melody Green."

That was a code we set up, it meant to bug out, or coms were compromised, only team guys listening in would know for sure its meaning. We had, of course, not used it before, so I am sure the boys at Alpha were breaking out their codebooks to figure out what was going on.

We started a fire, it was the only way we would be able to dry out our boots, but it had to be small. We had a few hours of daylight left; we would make our way back through the woods at dusk to the new recon point. We had to remember that if we killed even one member of their group, we would be hunted until we were caught or killed. I took the first watch at this point. The adrenaline was wearing off, so my feet were getting cold, and I mean COLD. It took better than an hour before Two-Five started to put his socks back on, and damn, that was a beautiful sight. It meant my turn was coming soon. Once I sat down, I didn't think my feet would ever warm back up.

At dusk, we smothered our fire and started to make movement to the house. We followed the creek bed back until we found our escape tracks, then we slowed our pace even more; booby traps were now a legitimate fear. The closer we got, we could hear people talking. We looked through the trees and could see that they had posted a couple of guards at the spot we had been watching them from. We snuck through, making our way to the back of the house. We hopped through a window and up a set of stairs to the second floor. We found a room that had a good view of the prison entrance and thankfully, glass still in the windows to shield us from the wind.

We got out notebooks so we could write down what we saw. I don't think anything in the world could have prepared us for what we would be witness to for the next twenty-four hours. The prison was lit up like a Christmas tree. Best guess was they wanted to keep it lit up in case we came back and tried to scale the prison walls to infiltrate.

Out from the main entrance door walked a dark skin man in a prison jumpsuit. He looked malnourished and had three teardrop looking tattoos down the right side of his face, just then the man who walked out with him held up a microphone which was for the prison loudspeaker.

"Tell everyone your name nigger" he said.

"John," he struggled to speak. "Johnny Stevens," said the inmate, he was shaking and could barely stand.

"Well, everyone, here's Johnny," laughed the white guy. "He is going to start tonight's monthly fire."

He handed Johnny a can of gas and shoved him towards the small snow-covered mound. Focusing on the mound and the parking lot being completely lit, I could see an arm sticking from the middle of the pile. Johnny climbed on top of the pile and began pouring the gas. Once he climbed down, he was given a road flair, which he lit, throwing it on the pile starting the fire. As the fire grew, the smell of burning flesh filled the air. The entire mound was made up of dead inmates. The smell made my stomach turn. I could tell by the look on Two-Five's face; it was taking everything inside him not to start taking those sick bastards off this earth. He could tell I felt the same. They took Johnny Stevens back inside the prison.

I told him to get some rest, we would have to break up the night watch, or at some point, we would both fall asleep, though I knew it would be hard for us both to rest with the smell of death in the air. Shortly after, I could hear him faintly snoring; there was a guard shift, not just at the prison but at our previous hide as well. The shift did not go smoothly; however, as the two guards came to the house, we were in, looking for the other guards. They must have seen them over where we had been because they walked over and started talking to them. When the conversation was over, the new guards returned to the front of the house and walked into the downstairs. I could hear them talking.

"I can't believe those stupid fuckers thought they were supposed to stand over there, the guys that were watching would see them, they should have known to be over here." one guard said to the other.

They continued talking through the night. They kept going on about their excitement over the morning festivities. I woke Two-Five, probably not the best idea to rest when either of us could potentially snore loud enough to get our asses busted. When the sun started to show itself, we began packing our gear quietly, so as not to alert our uninvited guests. We did not make any coffee or chow for the very same reasons.

We got back to intel gathering; we saw so much more than the floodlights had let us see through the night. They seemed to have a lot of military issue Humvees; some had 50 caliber machine guns mounted on them, others had 240 machine guns. This may explain why we never saw any national guard or state troopers as the early reports suggested we should have. We saw a large tent at the north end. It looked to be where they kept their ammunition stored.

"I thought the Goldbeach guard unit had three times as many Humvees as what is sitting there," said Two-Five.

"They did, which means that someone else has the rest," I replied.

We watched as thirty to forty men and women walked out the front entrance making their way to the center of the parking lot. They started lifting a frame of sorts off the ground and assembling it. Gallows, it was a set of gallows that they put together. Once finished, it looked as though they were placing bets with each other. The front door opened, again, out walked Johnny Stevens with probably the same piece of shit white guy as the night before with the microphone in his hand.

"Ok everyone, time to place your bets, does the nigger break his neck or does he hang until his death?" he said.

I heard the sound of the safety on the rifle drop. I turned to see Two-Five getting ready to take the shot.

"What the fuck are you doing?" I asked.

"I'm going to face shoot that mother fucker," he said.

"You can't do that," I said.

"We can't let them do this; it's not right," he said.

"I agree, brother, you know damn well I do, but if you pull that trigger, we will be caught and killed, remember there is two of them below us, maybe we can take them, but we will not get out of here in time to outrun the rest of them," I said frantically.

"What are we if we let him die like that?" he asked with tears in his eyes.

"We are two soldiers, two that need to make it home so we can tell the team what we saw here, so we can figure out how to come back here and kill every last one of those mother fuckers." I said.

He did not like my answer, but he knew I was right. He put the rifle back on safe. I turned and looked into the scope just as Johnny Stevens fell to his death. He did not struggle long; his body was too week to fight to survive. I moved my scope off, Johnny; I could not bear to watch him die. I gave my attention to the south wall, where I finally saw the primary reason we returned to the prison in the first place. Sally in the flesh. It looked as though he was using his military experience to help guide the crazy whites on how to be "squared away."

It was time now to get out of the area. It was going to be very challenging since we had company below. I got up super slowly, making my way to the door. Two-Five looked at me like I was losing my mind. Once I got to the door, I turned and put my back to the wall inside the door; I then took an extra pistol mag from its pouch and threw it across the room, hitting the wall. Two-Five began to panic as we could hear one of the guards coming up the stairs. Two-Five watched as I pulled my field knife from its sheath. The guard came to the door, making eye contact with Two-Five; before he could say a word, my hand was over his mouth, pulling him into me as my knife punched into his neck. His blood sprayed all over the wall and my arm. Once the life left his body, I signed to Two-Five to make his way downstairs. He crept past me slowly, once in the hallway, he walked down the stairs like normal.

"Is everything ok?" asked the other guard.

A few moments later, I was given the all-clear. I dropped the body and finished packing our hide for a speedy getaway. Two-Five had not returned, so I started to carry our gear downstairs myself, I got to the bottom, and Two-Five was standing there over the body of the second guard with his boot on his neck.

"Please get the zip cuffs and gorilla tape from my bag," he said.

"You have zip cuffs?" I asked.

"You mean, you don't? I bought the fuckers from you," he said with a chuckle.

I handed him what he asked for, he stood the guard up, zip cuffing his hands above his head in a doorway that had a hole over the frame, and he taped his mouth shut.

"We need to go," I said.

"Not yet, I'm not done with this piece of shit," he said.

He turned to the guard taking out his knife "you think it's fun, you think it is cool to torture and starve a man because of the color of his skin?" he asked the guard who was mumbling through the tape in tears.

"You think betting on their death is fun?" he asked.

He slowly began to push his knife into the guard's liver, removing it before pushing it back in. The guard screamed in pain through the tape.

"Look at me you sick Nazi fuck," he said as he grabbed the guard by his face "I bet it takes twenty to thirty minutes for you to die here,

alone, in the worst pain of your life, how much is that bet worth?"
he asked

CHAPTER 14

We finished grabbing our gear and got ready to head out. I did not blame Two-Five for choosing to kill that guard in the manner he did; all of those sick bastards deserved that and so much more. Just then, I saw two females of military fighting age headed toward the house.

"We need to move NOW!" I said.

We made our way out the back door; we were only fifty feet from the door when we could hear the women screaming for help. We made a straight line to the creek bed again; we could hear the crazy whites, but it did not sound like they were following us yet. As we approached the creek bed, I turned again to check our six when suddenly I heard Two-Five groaning in pain. I turned back and made my way to find him lying in the creek holding his ankle.

"What the fuck happened?" I asked.

"My foot slipped on that rock when I hopped down and rolled my ankle," he said.

"What is that? All of a twenty-inch drop? How fucking retarded do you have to be to get hurt on such a small drop?" I asked, chuckling.

"Fuck you, asshole, help me up so we can get the fuck out of here," he said.

I slung Black Betty on my back and helped his big ass up, putting his arm around my neck to help him walk. We moved as fast as we could, still with no sounds of being followed. We walked for a couple of hours before getting out of the creek bed, making our way into the woods for some rest. We made it maybe a mile. At this rate, we were going nowhere fast. We built another really small fire again to dry out our boots.

Two-Five, as best as he could, stood the first watch while I dried out my boots. Once they were dry enough, I slipped them back on.

"You think we're in the clear?" I asked.

"Yeah, why what you are thinking?" he asked.

"I think that I should move ahead and see what is in front of us, better to find the right path to take, then be surprised and wind up in a gunfight with you broken and stupid," I said.

"Fuck you," he said.

"Here is a SAM splint, try to stabilize that ankle before I return," I told him as I walked away.

I didn't want to leave him if the Nazis were being quiet and looking for us, then he would be in a bad way, but we both felt positive about not being followed. If they were sneaky, however, I hope he would not let them take him alive. I went through the south side of the woods, headed back towards town. I cut east on my way, heading back towards the gas station. I figured it would be a great place to hold up for the night. I got to the houses on the outskirts of town. I made my way between them slowly, trying to make sure I did nothing to draw attention to myself. I got to a house roughly thirty yards from the station on the opposite side of the road. I could see movement and that all too familiar Nazi truck from days before. I stayed hidden and watched as the crazy whites appeared to be working alongside the Red X gang. They were pointing at the station as if telling them someone had overwatch on them days earlier.

I had spent enough time there; I needed to get back to Two-Five. I turned to leave when I saw a child's sled; it was themed from the child's movie Frozen. It gave me an idea, so I took it and continued making my way back to Two-Five. I dropped the sled five yards from where he sat.

"See anything worth talking about?" he asked.

"Yeah, it looks like the crazy whites and the Red X boys are working together, probably to find us."

"Fucking charming news that is," he said.

"I have an idea, I found a sled, you sit in it with our gear, and I'll pull you behind me," I said.

"That's a good idea," he said.

"There's a catch," I said.

"What," he asked.

"It's from the movie Frozen," I told him.

"You're such a fucking dick," he said.

"It was all I could find to help," I told him as I walked back to get it laughing.

When I brought it back, he started rigging 550 cord to it long enough to wrap around my waist, keeping a fair amount of distance between us in case, for some reason, I fell. We started heading to the west side of center to make our way home. We were making slightly better time. We got a half-mile within the hour; however, I was getting more tired, dragging him behind me.

"Have your trainees been sneaking extra food for you?" I asked.

"What the fuck is that supposed to mean?" he asked.

"You, sir, are fat," I said.

"Fuck you, I'm not fat," he said.

"Seriously, I have no idea how the fuck you can even walk, FATTY," I said, laughing.

"Fuck you asshole, both of our god damn bags are back here with me," he said.

"Yours is probably full of snacks," I said.

"I swear to Christ, I'm going to shoot you in the back," he said in a very pissy tone.

"Why is that? You getting hungry?" I asked.

"Fuck you, I'm not fat, asshole," he yelled.

"Says the fat fuck in the sled being dragged behind me," I laughed.

"Fuck you. I'm in the sled because I hurt my ankle, you fucking ASSHOLE," he said.

"Maybe we should sing to pass the time," I suggested.

"What the fuck are you talking about?" he asked.

"You know, like when you were a kid, riding in the car with your parents and you sang as a family," I said.

"You seriously need medication," he told me.

"Let it go. Let it go." I started to sing.

"I swear to fucking god I will kill you," he said.

"Don't hold it back anymore; let it go, let it go." I continued to sing.

"I am turning my radio back on, so I can talk to someone with intelligence," he said.

"Turn it on for sure, just no transmitting, they are probably still listening, and we do not want them figuring out our position," I said.

"Yeah, that makes sense," he replied.

"See, I is be smart and shit," I said, laughing.

"You're still a fucking man child," he said.

"AND my kids love it!! It is not my fault you're a whiney little bitch." I said.

"I am not whiney; you just pick the absolute worst times to be a total child," he said.

"The worst times are the best times," I replied.

We both laughed as we clicked on our radios. It didn't take long to hear Six-One come over the speaker.

"Six-Eight, Six-Eight this is Six-One if you can hear this, there is a big storm coming in, word on the short wave says it will be here by nightfall, advise you seek shelter immediately, God be with you," he said.

Every thirty minutes or so, Six-One came over the radio with the same message. He knew from our last call we could not radio back; even hearing the worry in his voice, it was best to remain radio silent on our end until we were much closer to home. We were four miles from home; if Two-Five were healthy, it would take a full day in decent weather, but shit weather and having to pull his fat ass, it was going to be at least two days before we were home, which meant at least one day with no food.

It was getting dark when we got far enough into the woods that I was no longer worried about anyone seeing us. I started building a shelter for the night, under the supervision of Two-Five, he was far better at bushcraft than I was, even with instruction, it was not easy for me being on a deadline. The snow moved in quickly. I was able to not only finish the shelter but also get the fire going before things got too nasty outside.

"How's the ankle?" I asked Two-Five as I settled in.

"It hurts but nowhere near as bad as it was," he said.

"That's good to hear, get some rest," I said.

"You rest first, no one is going to come looking for us in this weather, and you need the rest more than I do." He said.

"Yeah, pulling your fat ass has been exhausting, that's for sure," I said laughing.

"Fuck you," he said.

I laughed as I put my back to the fire to get some rest. I shut my eyes for what only seemed like a few minutes when I woke in a complete panic from the dream I had. Two-Five could tell something was wrong.

"Want to talk about it pussy?" he asked.

"Not with you, fatty," I said.

"Coffee," he held a cup up to me.

"Yeah, how long was I out for?" I asked.

"About ten hours and you were snoring like a mother fucker" he said.

"From the look of things outside, the weather didn't let up either, did it?" I asked.

"Not even a little, Six-One came over the air about ten minutes ago, the weather is supposed to be this shitty through tonight too, so we won't be moving until tomorrow," he said.

"Fuck," I said.

"Well, let me make your day a little brighter, I just made the last of the coffee, and we have enough instant oatmeal for one more meal each," he said.

"Jesus Christ! Maybe I should go back to sleep, wake up, and try this fucking day over again," I said.

At this point, I must have zoned out some.

"Hey, fucker did you hear me?" he asked.

"Sorry, what?" I asked.

"Seriously, I am getting worried, you ok, brother?" he asked.

"Not really," I said.

"Tell me what is on your mind. A distracted soldier is a dead soldier," he said.

"That dream I had, all I can remember is getting into a gunfight with those Nazi fucks, they used a 50 Cal and shot towards my house, when the fight ended, I ran to the house. When I got inside, all I could hear was screaming from the upstairs, and when I got up there, Ann was standing outside Princess' room. As I opened the door, the room was destroyed, and my kids were ripped apart by that 50," I said.

"Shit, no wonder you're more fucked up than normal, brother I know better, you will keep your kids safe, fuck you keep everyone safe," he said.

"Yeah, I hope so," I said.

"Listen, whether anyone including myself has liked it or not, you have always done what has been in the best interest of the team and of the group, keep faith in yourself, brother, the way we have all kept our faith in you," he said.

"Wilco, now what did you say when I zoned out?" I asked.

"We need more wood if we are going to stay warm through this shit," he said as he dug a finger saw out from his bag.

I took it from him and made my way outside to find us some wood. I looked for wood that was above the ground, least likely to be soaked that way entirely. If not for the blistering wind, it would have almost been peaceful being out in the storm. Unfortunately, however, it gave me too much time to think about my dream, but Two-Five was right, I got this.

It took a couple of hours before I returned with enough wood for the day, dragging it behind me in the sled. I crawled back into the shelter to find Two-Five sound asleep. I fed the fire slowly so it would build back up warm and not go out on us. I wrote out all the extra information my field reports needed. I used the rest of my time to think about my kids, the things I should have done differently in life, differently to prepare, but once I started to second guess my abilities as the team leader, I quickly put my focus elsewhere. Three hours had past when I heard the wind finally die down. I popped my head out of the shelter to see that the storm had stopped. It was comforting that even in such times, the idiots reporting on the weather were still full of shit. I looked at my watch; we had five hours of good light left; if we left now, we would get that much closer to home.

I woke Two-Five, we got our gear together and were making movement within thirty minutes towards home. The snow was deep; even with my snowshoes on, it was hard to walk in, let alone dragging fatty behind me, but we had to move as much as we could. It was three hours when the struggle started to get to me. With only two hours or so of daylight left, we could not stop now. I was getting tired. It was getting harder to lift my legs, hard to breathe. I pulled my face mask down, breathing the cold air in deep, which burned my lungs. Two-Five asked if I wanted a break, I told him no, though I wanted to.

I dropped to my knees, unable to continue, just then I could see my kids, they were so excited to see me. It took everything I had inside me to get up. Every step I took towards them, they seemed to take a step backward. They started cheering me on, telling me I could do it. This went on and on. I told them to stop, I just wanted hugs and kisses, but they kept moving back, giggling. It was almost dark before I knew it, "See you soon, daddy," my kids said as they faded into the nothing. Two-Five directed me to an area where it would be easy to set up a quick shelter. Once set, he started melting snow to help get me hydrated.

"You were hallucinating, bad brother," he said.

"The kids were right here," I said, looking around.

"Brother, you need to drink water and get some rest," he said.

"But the kids, where did they go?" I asked.

"We are within two miles of home; they went back to wait there for you, brother," he said to humor me.

Once the water was ready, I started to drink it. I must have drunk too fast as I started to cough. I could feel a burning in my chest from the cold.

"Sip it slow, asshole, last thing I need, is you dying on me." He said.

I sipped for a few more minutes, then dozed off for the night. Everyone says Mother Nature is a bitch, well in western New York, she must have multiple personality disorder because when we woke, it had to be near forty degrees outside, not bad for the beginning of February. We packed quickly and waited until 10 am, for the sun to be bright before we moved. Being closer to home, we decided to open communications back up with Alpha; however, we did not want to use our previous code for fear of who might still be listening.

"I am looking for tickets to the next Yankees game," I said over the radio, "I say again, I am looking for tickets to the next Yankees game."

"Only tickets I have is for the races," said a familiar voice over the radio.

"This is Mr. Green, who am I speaking with," I asked.

"This is Mr. Blue," replied Six-One. Mr. Blue was a backup call-sign for him.

"We are two miles southeast of your position, ETA midpoint of the day, Mr. Green out," I said.

We moved as fast as we could. There wasn't one cloud in the sky, which made the sun gleam extra bright off the snow, add to that the knee-deep snow it took near five hours to get to Alpha. Once there, I instantly grabbed an MRE, ripped it open, and began eating.

"Where's Three-Three," I asked.

"Here, boss," he said as he came from the back, tripping over himself to get to me.

"Go find my dad, tell him Two-Five has an ankle that needs looked at right now, and stay the fuck off your radio," I said.

"Wilco boss," he said as he took off towards Main.

I finished eating, stripped off my gear, and changed while waiting on Doc to arrive. One-Three came up with a change of clothes for Two-Five. I sent Six-One down to get Two-Eight to come to Alpha. Doc looked over Two-Five telling him to stay off his feet for a few days, giving him an air cast to help stabilize his ankle. I briefed the rest of the team on the events they missed when we went radios silent. Once briefed, everyone returned to their perspective team locations.

I left Alpha, making my way down to Main. It was 8 o'clock by then. I walked in the door, and there stood my wife. I had never been so happy to see her. She, on the other hand, wasn't so happy to see me.

"Where the fuck have you been?" she asked.

"Up at Alpha like I told you," I said.

"Bullshit, I did some snooping around, and I never saw you up there. I also have not seen your ex in as many days," she said with a very pissed off tone.

"And here the fuck we go again," I said.

"I know you're lying, so you may as well tell me," she growled.

"Since you are not going to be pleasant, I am going to go find my kids," I said.

"The fuck you are, stand here like the man you think you are and tell me the truth," she demanded.

"Ok, you want the truth, here it is, Ricky and I went uptown to see what evils are lurking in the shadows that we know nothing about. We saw evil in its most pure form. We saw things that history should have never allowed itself to repeat, things that would cause you never to sleep again. Especially knowing that on any given day, those evils could be knocking on the doors of this very fucking house. Yes, I lied, why because you don't want to know what we do to keep your ass safe, and once again, I am greeted at my fucking door with your bullshit," I barked.

"What do you mean?" she asked with genuine fear in her voice.

"I mean I'm fucking tired, I'm sore, I'm horrified as to the things I've seen, and I need to see the faces of those that love me. You obviously don't wish to be in that category tonight, so I will go see my kids now," I said as I walked past her.

I went up to our bedroom to find my kids asleep, Handsome, half on his bed half under mine, Princess, curled up with her head on my pillow. I stood watching them when Princess sat up, looking at me.

"Dada, are you coming to bed?" she asked.

I smiled, walked over to the bed, wrapping her in my arms as I laid down and drifted off for the night.

CHAPTER 15

I was violently awoken by a thirty-eight-pound princess pouncing on my stomach, indeed not what I was expecting; however, I could not think of a better way to be woke up. I made my way down to the stove, with Princess in my arms. Making my coffee, I set her down and made her some breakfast while waiting for my brew. I set her breakfast on the table for her, cut myself a cigar, she asked if she could smell it before I lit it, rolling it under her nose, handing it back to me," it smells like a good one, dada." I sat sipping my coffee, watching her eat. I looked up to see Three-Three coming through the door.

"Morning boss, morning Princess," he said. "Six-One sent me down to see if there was anything you needed to be done this morning?"

"It's like he read my mind; I was thinking based on the intel we gathered, I would like you to go tell One-Three to send Ryan, Robbie, and their family down to join Charlie team in the event of an attack," I said.

"Wilco boss," he said as he turned for the door.

"Wait for one," I said, "Did you eat yet? Do you want some coffee? A cigar?" I asked.

"No, thanks, boss. I'm good for now," he said.

"You sure?" I asked.

"Yeah, I don't drink coffee," he said.

"Makes since being a liberal and all," I said, laughing.

He laughed as he walked out the door. I continued to watch Princess eat. She would stop occasionally, look at me and smile, sometimes she would stick her tongue out at me, and a few times, I was extra lucky because she started singing. She always loved to sing. I was not long before my wife and Handsome walked down the stairs. She walked over, taking my empty mug, walked into the kitchen and returned with a second cup for me and one for herself, as my son sat at the table with the breakfast he got.

"Thank you, Mama," I said.

"You're welcome," she said.

"Bubby, Bubby, Bubby look Dada is home," said Princess.

"I know," he said as he stood up and hugged me.

"Not sure what bullshit, people are claiming for the weather. It's already sunny out, and Three-Three came down here in a hoodie," I said, looking at my wife.

"Do you think since it is warm out, that people will try to attack us again?" asked my wife.

Suddenly my son looked up and started crying, "I don't want people to kill us," he screamed through his tears.

"That's why we do not talk about this shit in front of the kids," I said, looking at my wife. I turned to my son, taking him into my arms. "Daddy is here, no one is going to hurt you, your sister or anyone here so long as I can pull the trigger, I will keep you safe," I told him.

"But mommy said that people were going to attack us," he cried.

"Momma asked if people would try, if they do, I'll kill them, I'll kill them all, I will burn this world to the ground to keep you safe," I told him.

"Ok," he said as he wiped away his tears, using my shirt.

"You good Handsome?" I asked him.

He shook his head yes, turned, and walked from the room. Princess followed him out. I could hear them beginning to play in the next room when Three-Three came running through the door. He was gasping for air, unable to speak.

"Relax, asshole, or you're going to pass out," I told him.

"They need you at Alpha RIGHT NOW!!!!" he said once he caught his breath.

I got up, walked upstairs, got on my field gear, grabbed Betty, headed back downstairs, and out the door we went. His urgency could only mean one thing. I, however, didn't walk fast on my way to Alpha. We trained our shooters well. If they couldn't handle it without me, we were screwed anyway. Most of the snow on the road had melted over the last two days, so it did not take us long to get there. Robin was on the bolt gun, Six-One was looking through a spotting scope both towards the farm and Charlie team.

"What's going on?" I asked.

"The fuck, you stop for coffee or something?" asked Six-One.

"No, I finished the cup I had, so there was no need to stop on my way," I said, smiling.

"We have uninvited guests," said Robin.

Six-One was sure one of them was Sally, so I took the scope from him to confirm that it was, in fact, him. It was a driver and a 240 gunner that accompanied him. They arrived at the farm in a military issue Humvee that had Nazi flags draped on the hood and sides of it. Sally appeared to be talking to Two-Eight, who had him at gunpoint, with his hands in the air. I told Six-One to get me a pen and paper. I wrote a message on it and handed it to Three-Three.

"You run as fast as your ass can back to Bravo, you give this paper to Two-Five, don't try and speak because that will take way to long, just give him this fucking paper," I said to him.

He turned and took off running. I took off my gear leaving only my battle belt on with my pistol. I mounted my radio to the back of it, turning it on and put in my earpiece. Then I put on a hoodie that was sitting there for a bit of warmth.

"That's mine," said Robin in a pissy tone.

"It fits well, thank you, good thing your tits are huge and stretched it out," I said.

"What did the paper say?" asked Six-One.

"It said for Two-Five and One-Three to get the other bolt gun the fuck down here and for them to both be setup on one. It said to turn on their radios, to get the gunner and driver in their crosshairs. When they do, they break squelch three times. That lets me know they are ready to engage. You will be on the spotter scope. When you see me light a cigar, you give them the green light to shoot," I said.

Six-One asked what I was going to do. I smiled. I was going to have a talk with our dear old friend Sally. I started to walk towards the farm. I figured by the time I arrived down there; the boys should be in place. I did take my time, almost no snow in the road, yet the earth all-around was still covered and honestly quite beautiful. The closer I got, the more clearly, I could hear Two-Eight screaming at Sally and his friends to leave or die. Sally looked as expected, wearing Multicam BDUs, a cheap Chinese Multicam plate carrier with way more mags than any one man could need, what looked like a Sig P226 in an even cheaper nylon drop leg holster, and nice new looking pair of Salomon shoes. He always believed if he looked the part, people wouldn't realize he never actually trained for it.

I got there, and the first mission was to settle Charlie team down; before things escalated out of control, they lowered their weapons and went back to their posts. Next, I got Sally to get the gunner to take his finger off the trigger and for his driver to step out of the hummer, for my safety as well as his own.

"What the fuck do you want, Sally?" I asked.

"First, I told you and your asshole buddies not to fucking call me that. Second, we are here because you or Ricky killed my boss' son," he said.

"No clue what you're talking about," I said.

He threw a Losers team patch at me. "I was in the bar when Ricky's cousin Turbo was telling people about your stupid boy's club, he like everyone there, thought a bunch of grown-ass men having a special club was stupid, we found that patch on the boss' kids body. Now I know you two are tight, and I saw Ryan here, which means Ann is here too, and everyone knows how much you hated Ryan for taking Ann from you, so put the two five patch on him, kill him and let us take his body back to my boss. If not, we return without a body; the boss will mobilize a small army to come and wipe you off this fucking earth," he told me.

"I never figured you would tag in with such shitty people, I mean you're a fucking asshole piece of shit, but I never thought you were that big of one. I figured you would have held up with that Puerto Rican kid and his family, Sisco was his name if I recall, right?" I said, just then, I heard the radio squelch three times.

"Yeah, well, he understood I had to do what was necessary to survive. Are you going to hand over Ryan, or are we coming back with the full force of our army to kill you?" he asked.

"You want me to give up one of my team, to satisfy your boss? A very sick and twisted psychopath. I can say I honestly never liked the fucker, but not enough to sell my soul to your boss," I said as I pulled my cigar out of my pocket, cutting it.

"Fuck, you're one stupid mother fucker, even my boss negotiated with the fucking blacks since this war started, so don't be so stupid, take this fucking deal," he said.

"Sally, what happened to Sisco?" I asked as I leaned into lighting my cigar.

"I said not to fucking call me that, call me that again, and I will tell these guys to kill you!!!!" he shouted at me.

Just then, the subsonic crack from the rifles being fired broke the sound barrier, the 240 gunner fell back inside the hummer, and the driver fell onto the road. Both were good clean kill shots. Sally stumbled, falling over.

"FUCK" he screamed, "What the fuck, Will what the fuck did you do?"

"Now, Sally, let us begin negotiating, shall we?" I asked.

"Will, we have to be back in one hour with a body. If the three of us didn't return or return with a body, they are going to mobilize on this position," he said sobbing as he brought himself up to a knee.

"Don't get up; you are fine on your knees," I said as Charlie team ran out to watch the show.

"Will please, I'm begging you," sobbed Sally.

"Tell me, Sally, the deal your boss made with the blacks, as you put it, was it with the group held up at the hotel? What the fuck could they have given him?" I asked.

"The deal was with the head of the X boys, and they're in Goldbeach when my boss took the prison over the Head of the X boys' brother was in the prison. So, they traded his life for weapons and trucks that they had stolen from the guard unit. His brother did not want to go to Goldbeach, he wanted his own territory, so they held up at the old hotel. There was also an agreement to leave his brother alone, or the X boys would come to annihilate the whites. They have far more firepower than we do," he continued to sob.

"Now tell me, what the fuck happened to Sisco," I asked.

"We were bugging out, headed to PA when we were found outside the prison, and they told me if I killed them, it would prove my loyalty to my race" he began to cry like a six-year-old getting beat in Kmart.

"Them, what the fuck do you mean them?" I asked.

"Sisco, his wife, and son, it was the only way to survive," cried Sally.

"The only way to survive. You sold the life of the only person I knew of who still said you were a good person, the only guy I knew who still called you his friend in public, the only guy I knew of who still actually liked you. You're telling me that you're such a coward you sold his life and the lives of his wife and son for your own? He would have taken a bullet for you, and you wouldn't even take one with him? You gave their lives to be a slave, a slave to the very same group of men that would kill you for calling him a friend. You asked me to sell out Ryan because I hate him, and I will admit I am not very fond of the fucker, but he is on my team because he earned the right to fight by my side, and I will take a bullet for him if it is necessary. You wanted me to choose the same slavery you chose," I said as I unholstered my pistol.

"Will no, please, I am begging," cried Sally.

"I choose life. You can suffer for your sins," I said as I shot him in the throat.

He fell over, holding his throat as he choked to death on his blood. I watched as the life left his body and his eyes started to glaze. It was a different feeling for me. Killing someone I know from my now former life, but he already had no soul, maybe I just did his body a favor.

Most of the team walked away while I stood there. Two-Eight, Ryan and Robbie were still standing there when I finally looked up.

"What now?" asked Two-Eight.

"I have no fucking idea, Sally said that the crazy whites would mobilize in an hour, that was fifteen minutes ago," I said when Robbie interrupted me.

"What the fuck do you mean they're going to mobilize" asked Robbie in a panic. "We will never beat their army; you should have just fucking gave up, Ryan."

I was not surprised that Robbie would be willing to sell out his brother-in-law, before dating his sister, when we were still friends, he admitted to me how much he despised him

"They would've left us alone, now what the fuck are we going to do?" asked Robbie again.

"Fuck you, Robbie, how the fuck can you suggest selling me out to those fuckers? I'm your fucking brother-in-law, the father of your nephew," Ryan said as he slugged Robbie in the face. The two of them brawled for a couple of minutes before Six-Six broke it up.

"You find out real quick during a time like this who your true family is and who the cowards are," I said to Ryan. I then turned my attention to Robbie. "First, we will not now or ever sell out a teammate, if selling him out is your best idea, turn in your weapons, your gear, take your wife and get the fuck away from the rest of us because you will most certainly get one or more of us killed," I said to Robbie.

I stared at the truck as everyone around me seemed to be panicking a bit, when suddenly it hit me, what if we did not have to fight them at all? I thought as I stared at the 240-machine gun.

I turned to Two-Eight "How much training do you have on that weapon" I asked him, pointing at the 240. "Can you give Six-Six a crash course in its operation?" I asked.

"Yes, I can, what are you thinking, boss?" he asked.

"Get to teaching Six-Six what he needs to know, and I mean yesterday," I told him.

"Wilco boss, Six-Six get your big ass up there once you help me get that dead piece of shit out of the back," he yelled.

I hit the push to talk button on my radio "One-Three radio check over."

"I hear you, brother, what you need?" he asked.

"Grab both bolt guns, my field gear, Betty and get your ass the fuck down here fast; we have business to handle."

"Copy that," he said.

Two-Five came over the radio. "Can someone take Sally's Salomons off and bring them up to me? I always wanted a pair, they'd fit better with this air cast, and besides, he doesn't need them anymore."

Two-Eight and I just looked at each other laughing before he told Robbie to take the shoes to Two-Five

It took an additional ten minutes before One-Three was at the farm. I threw on my gear and had him load the rifles in the back of the truck, after which he linked two of the 240 ammo belts together and gave them back to Two-Eight, who had just finished up showing Six-Six all he would need to know. I told One-Three to get his ass in the driver's seat and for Six-Six to sit until we were close to where we were going.

I turned to Two-Eight before getting into the hummer. "You sure he is good to go on that weapon system."

"Fuck, yes, he is, but why not just let me go and run that fucker" asked Two-Eight.

"Honestly, brother, you're not white enough for what's about to happen," I said, laughing as I got in.

CHAPTER 16

I wasn't a great plan, but it was still a plan. We did have to fix one thing before we pulled away; however, I called Two-Eight back over to the vehicle. We started stripping off team patches and our wedding rings. Anything that could identify us had to go in case we were seen, caught, or involved in an up-close altercation like before. Once all was handed over, we took off down the road; time was critical. When we got about a mile from the farm, I turned to Six-Six and explained what I wanted him to do.

"On my go, you open fire on the hotel, both floors. However, you need to shoot above their heads as best as you can. We're not trying to kill anyone so much as we're trying to kick a hornet's nest," I told him.

He nodded his head, understanding. We made the necessary turns needed to be coming up on the hotel from the west like we had seen the Nazi truck do before. The closer we got, it seemed the more One-Three was white knuckle driving. I think the silence may have been bothering him the most.

"Relax, brother, when we get close drift into the opposite lane, this should help create enough space for him to shoot above their heads on the second floor. You stay in the truck; I'll get out and provide any cover fire he may need" I told him

He nodded as well, that is when I figured out it was not the silence getting to them, but the fact it was both their first time out, and this was a very up close and personal mission, certainly not what either of them had had to do so far. I must admit that realization had me a bit nervous at that point also, but I knew my plan would bring them home alive. What I did not know, what couldn't possibly be foreseen, was that this moment would define the events that happened in the future.

We drifted into the opposite lane; Six-Six stood up, getting the 240 ready chambering the first round. The truck started slowing down when finally, it came to a stop in front of the hotel. I could feel my heart beating so hard. I could damn near hear it. I paused before getting out of the truck, checking the chamber on Betty. The X boys stood, staring at us, weapons down; they had no clue what was about to happen.

I got out of the truck, snapped the safety off Betty, started bringing her into my chest, and yelled NOW!!!! Six-Six began short bursts of fire into the hotel's first floor. The second-floor guards finally got brave enough to pop their heads up and try to shoot; I engaged them, killing one for sure. Six-Six switched his focus to the second floor, continuing the havoc. Once the gun ran dry, he dropped back inside the truck, I climbed in, and One-Three hammered on the gas, making a left-hand turn instantly.

Once we were far enough to be out of sight, we turned down one of the side streets, then turning on another, the plan now was to bring the hummer around and come in from the south of center. I instructed One-Three to turn the truck around. We could use the bed of it as a shooting platform. We got out and started setting up the bolt guns in the back, getting laid out, and ranging the town center. We were approximately twelve hundred yards out. Shots that far would be a challenge for us, neither of us had fired from that distance before, so we agreed it would be best to engage the same target when the time came. Six-Six began reloading the 240 for just in case we needed it again. According to Sally's time frame, we had ten minutes left before the Nazis would be on their way to us. We could only hope they'd take the main roads to us.

We watched as the X boys scurried below when suddenly we could see the Nazi marked trucks coming down the road. Four trucks total, one in front had a 50-caliber machine gun mounted on top. I told One-Three that if the 50-gunner acted like he was going to use it, we had to take him out. The trucks came to a stop at the corner, and the X boys opened fire on them. The crazy whites exited their trucks and returned fire, and both were suffering losses. When the 50-gunner decided to act, so did we. We both fired, only one round made an impact; I knew it was not my round as I saw mine shatter the windshield. I adjusted just in time to shoot another round, hitting the other scumbag that was trying to" work the 50. We continued watching the carnage unfold. The rear Humvee started to try and pull away when we shot out its tires. It still pulled all the turns it had too and started driving away on its rims. The fight appeared to be over for now.

The X boys started stacking the bodies of their dead out in the back parking lot. One of the X boys walked out to the lead Humvee. We could hear him transmitting over the radio, calling for help from the big boss of the X boys, they informed him that his little brother had been killed at the hands of the Nazis held up in the prison nearby. I instructed Six-Six to strip off the Nazi flags from the truck and burn them. I heard him exit the truck.

"Um boss, we got a few people out here approaching the vehicle," he said.

Making sure One-Three would be good without me for a few, I exited the truck, turned, and saw several men and women approaching us. Some had guns; the others had improvised weapons.

"You're surrounded, give up now, or we will kill you," said an older man.

I kept my hands visible and walked slowly toward the crowd, turning to Six-Six.

"Burn those fucking flags; we don't need any more shit paper at Main," I said. Then I turned my attention back to the seemingly growing crowd. "I don't know who you think we are, but I promise all of you we're not here to hurt any of you," I said.

"I said, if you give up now, we will not kill you," repeated the older man.

"Please return to your homes, we're not here to have trouble with any of you, we came to cause problems for those that I am sure have caused harm to you all," I said.

"We will not tell you or your men again" shouted the older man when he was interrupted by a younger man, probably around my age

"Dad, no!!!" he shouted, "That's Will, from the surplus store."

The younger man was named Clay; he was a former Goldbeach city cop; he moved to Virginia, becoming a cop down there. I had never met him before though we were friends with some of the same people and wound up friends on social media, thank god he recognized me. Six-Six finally began burning the flags.

"Last, I heard you were living in Virginia. What the fuck did you come back here for?" I asked Clay.

"My family and I came up last summer for vacation so that the kids could see their grandparents. Then all fucking hell broke loose. It was easier to stay here than it was to try and get home," he said.

"Makes sense to me. How many do you have in your group?" I asked.

"There are twenty of us, and we are continually moving around the town to avoid detection, was that you we saw creeping around town last week?" He asked.

"Yeah, another guy and I, doing some recon to see what was going on around us, thought we were sneakier than we were apparently," I said.

"You guys did alright, had a feeling you weren't with any of the shitbag groups in town, nor with any of the groups I heard about in the surrounding towns," he laughed.

"You guys are welcome to join our group outside of town," I said.

"I appreciate the offer, but part of what we are doing is providing aid to those in need. Helping them fortify their homes, teaching some medical, even gave up some of our weapons to some women who had been raped by those Nazi fuckers on more than one occasion, that is why some of the group here are using improvised weapons," He said.

"Sounds like some doctors without borders type of shit," I said, laughing.

One-Three called for my attention; I ran back over to the truck. He could see somewhere near a dozen trucks stopping in front of the hotel. It must have been the X boys from Goldbeach picking up the survivors to go and fight with the Nazis. Once they were all loaded up, they turned the trucks and headed towards the prison. It didn't take long before we could hear the gunfire begin. We decided to move the truck ahead to bring us within eight hundred yards of town center.

Clay and I continued to talk about his mission. There were several small groups spread throughout the area, many of whom were still in need of help. One-Three called for my attention again. He wondered if we should raid the hotel for weapons, this would help Clay and his group. It was a good idea, so I took it back and ran it past Clay. I knew as a cop; he had some entry training and room-clearing training; he was the only one in his group with an AR. Clay, Six-Six, and I would make entry while One-Three sat on overwatch covering all that he could see.

We made entry; they had taken every one to help fight. We looked for weapons, medical supplies, food, and anything else the group could benefit from having. We found a small stash of ammunition, which we split between us and Clay's group. We got to the back of the hotel, still searching for things of use when we found the previous owner's office door. Inside was a massive stash of cocaine, heroin, methamphetamines, and an even bigger pile of money. Clay and I decided to split the money between our two groups. Understand that at this time, money was of no value at all, however in hopes, there would be an end to this war, it would be nice to use it to rebuild. I radioed for the truck to come down so we could load everything up. I walked out with the last load of stuff as Clay walked back inside.

"This is the last load, Clay," I said.

"I know, head back up, I'll be there in a minute," he said.

"We will wait here, provide you some cover," I said.

"Trust me, just go," he said.

We drove back to the top of the hill, one thousand yards from center. I got on the scope just in time to see Clay running for his life out of the back door. It didn't take long to see smoke coming from the hotel. Soon it was entirely on fire. I didn't ask him why he made that decision. I figured he had been hiding from them long enough and was just simply fed up. We drove a little further up the road to one of the hideouts that Clay used. We kept the spotting scope focused on the hotel.

We sat with Clay and his group, radioing back to Alpha, keeping sure to update them regularly. It was kind of nice to sit with different people. Clay said he'd planned to get a hold of me the week after the Cattleman's Ball so we could hang out. He even bought a box of cigars for the occasion, which he still had and gave me for our help. It was a box of Perdomo Estate Selection ESV; what a damn good smoke it was that evening. We stayed through the night, taking turns on overwatch, one of his guys and one of us. It came my turn for overwatch; Clay took his turn at that time as well. I fired up another cigar, trying to make the most of the moment. We talked a lot about everything and nothing at all when we could hear the gunfire from the direction of the prison finally start to die down. It took about ten minutes before some of the X Boys returned to find their headquarters still in flames. We could see the panic and confusion as it unfolded. We only paid enough attention to them after that to make sure they had no interest in coming towards us.

Morning came, we were getting ready to leave when I took Six-Six's radio and a portable solar charger giving them to Clay. I told him if he ever needed our help, he just had to call us, and we'd show up. He gave us a white flag with a blue painted on half-moon, he explained that it had become a symbol of hope. We were to use that flag anytime we decided to come back into town. It let other groups know that we were friendly; this way, they would not shoot at us if we got too close to their hideouts.

We pulled away; I offered One-Three and Six-Six a cigar, which they both accepted, it had been a while since either had enjoyed one, but with a very successful mission, in my opinion, they deserved one. On the drive back, we started to notice the flags, like the one we had been given, there was only five or six of them, but we did notice them. We were so focused on our previous mission that I wondered if they were there as we drove through the day before, or if they just went up because they somehow already knew we were friendly. We arrived back at the farm, made the call for all team leaders to meet so we could discuss the events that had taken place. I called for a team vote; I wanted to be sure that I had made the right decision based on the information obtained from Sally before his much-deserved death. No one objected to the call.

I walked my ass back to Main; I figured my wife would be again pissed off, especially since she had no idea what we had done, let alone the fact that I had left and was gone all night. Much to my surprise, I was greeted at the door with open arms. She told me that I was right; she had no clue the weight on my shoulders, trying to keep the group alive. She did ask one thing of me, to be honest about my movements and about what the world outside of our own looked like. I explained that sometimes, I wouldn't be able to relay my decisions before they happened. I then told her about my decision the day before after leaving the house. She did not take that so well; in fact, she was downright pissed off and stormed out of the room.

I made my way down to the cave; I needed a small drink while I filled out my reports. My wife came down a half-hour later. She wanted the details of my decision and our stay in town. She pulled a cigar from the humidor to smoke while I explained. With that information, she said she understood why we just left with zero notice to anyone. I didn't figure I was out of the woods with her yet, as she still seemed to have some attitude. I finished up my report, throwing the last drop of bourbon down the hatch as I stood up. I walked over, standing my wife up out of her chair, and began to dance with her, singing in her ear Sinatra's The way you look tonight. I felt her body relax in my arms so much, so she almost dropped her cigar. We continued to dance even after I stopped singing before we knew it, some thirty minutes had passed, and we heard the pitter-patter of little feet looking for us yelling, "Mama, Dada, where are you?"

We made our way upstairs, finding both kids playing in the living room. Dinner time came, and we went for chow as a family for the first time since the day of my grandpa's funeral. I think that made my kids day to have dinner as a family again. We went home, and I read to my kids for a couple of hours, neither of them wanted to go to bed since daddy was home, but they were both nodding off and asleep by the time I had finished. I insisted on carrying them both upstairs one at a time. Putting Handsome in his bed next to ours, then Princess in our bed. I put her on the side of the bed closest to my son. This way, mama could sleep next to me for once.

I went back downstairs and sat at the table when my wife walked in and sat down. She asked why we weren't doing something like what Clay and his group had been doing. Honestly, until she brought it up, it had not crossed my mind. I told her we could talk more about it in the morning, took her by the hand, walking her upstairs. We laid in bed, and she fell asleep with her head on my chest and her hand on my heart. I fell asleep with a smile on my face.

I awoke in the morning, around the time I usually did. Making my way down the stairs, brewing coffee, sitting at the table sipping my brew slowly thinking about what my wife had said the night before. I Called for the team leaders to meet me at Alpha within the hour so we could discuss the idea.

CHAPTER 17

I fixed a to-go cup of coffee for my wife while I waited for her to wake up. I wanted her to throw the idea to the team. She came downstairs, and we left for Alpha holding hands. Once we arrived, she brought the idea to life. My wife kissed me and walked back to Main, so I could "work," she said. I looked to the team once she left for a vote on the idea itself. Everyone voted yes. Now it was time to plan things out.

One-Three volunteered to check our inventory of weapons and ammo, to see if there was anything we could live without. I made my way back to the cave. I dug out some bottles of booze that we would never in our lifetime drink, mainly because the shit was that bad. I also dug out some pipe tobacco and cigars I knew we would never touch. Six-One went through our growing pile of animal hides. He figured some people would possibly want them for the making of clothing. Two-Eight and Six-Six did a count of what animals were left. They thought maybe if we had to, we could send a pig or cow off for trade.

We all met back at Alpha with a count on whatever we could spare. Now that we had that part figured out, we needed to figure out where we should go first. Looking at the map, the closest group we identified on our way home was only a mile away from the farm; we decided it made sense to start there. We started packing the hummer with what we had gathered when One-Three suggested that we perhaps wait until we found out what the group could use, and possibly what they could offer us before we just took stuff to their location. Six-One also suggested that maybe we leave the truck loaded, send a small team on foot, see what's needed, or can be traded then radio for the truck to send down stuff. These we both great ideas, and honestly, they came at the perfect time.

One-Three and Six-One offered to be the ground team. They would go and make introductions then radio for the truck. I headed up the vehicle team as the driver with Ryan as the 240 gunner and Three-Three as my passenger. We marked on the map at Alpha the route they would take, as well we marked spots where they would "check-in" over the radio just like we had seen on tv. As the ground team was getting ready to leave, Two-Eight asked if it would be best to send Robin with them. Having a woman go with might make introductions easier, especially if we came on the group of women that Clay had told us were held up together. Robin packed a go-bag and went off with the team. I then told Three-Three in the event of an emergency pick up we would need that seat empty, so he no longer had to go. I think he was relieved.

I stood by the truck, while Two-Eight gave Ryan a class on the use of the 240, smoking a cigar while we waited for word from the ground team. I was near done when One-Three came over the radio. He requested us to come down but did not request anything that we had set aside. We arrived at his location, and he walked over to me as I got out of the truck.

"These people have damn near all they need," he said.

"Then why call for the truck?" I asked.

"Because what they need, I wanted to talk to you face to face about, and if you wanted a team vote, then we could get back and vote quicker with the truck here than we could on foot," he said.

"Ok, what do they need?" I asked.

"Training and organization," he said.

Pulling guys to train others in the area, I did think, required a team vote. We left Six-One and Robin while we ran back to take a quick vote. One-Three had Six-One's proxy vote. It was voted yes to send a small group to give better weapons training to the local groups. Two-Five volunteered to do the training since he was off regular duties. I didn't think we needed to send anyone down for hand-to-hand combat training, the team agreed. We hopped back into the vehicle and ran Two-Five down to the first location. We explained that we would trade our ability to train the people for something. The group had a broke down tractor, so we traded training for what diesel fuel they had left, which amounted to about twenty gallons. The ground team would stay with him to provide security for the day while he trained the group. Once finished, they were to call for a ride home so we could resupply and move to the next known group.

We sat that evening, feeling just a little bit safer than we had in the past, knowing there was another group who at least had an eight-hour crash course in weapons handling was a nice thought. Two-Five came to the house that evening and asked if we should maybe give those folks another full day of instructions. It certainly couldn't hurt, the vote went to the team, and they all agreed. We decided from then forward; anyone who wanted training would get two days' worth for whatever they could spare to benefit our group.

We dropped off Two-five the next morning to continue training. Ryan and I stayed there with him to provide security while the ground team made their way from there to the next group, another mile and a half from there. It was about five hours before they returned to the first location with their assessment of what the next group needed and or wanted. Robin and I stayed while One-Three took Six-One and Ryan back to Alpha to get what was needed. They drove past us twenty minutes later to deliver and collect goods. When they came back to us, I looked at what we got. In the back of the vehicle was an antique hand-crank Retrola record player with a dozen records, including some Sinatra records.

"Why did you trade for that?" I asked.

"I figured we could put it up at the pavilion. People could then go there and listen to music if for no other reason than to relax their minds," he said.

"That makes sense. What did we have to trade to get it?" I asked.

"The old man said he missed being able to have a drink at the end of a hard day; he also missed the aroma of his pipe. I gave him two bottles, a bag of pipe tobacco, and one of Two-Five's pipes," He said.

"You gave away one of his pipes?" I asked.

"Yeah, do me a favor and don't tell him," ok?" he asked.

"Depends, how much is that information worth to you," I laughed.

"Asshole," he laughed.

"Why was the old man willing to give that up?" I asked.

"He had two," he said.

Honestly, from where I was standing, it was possibly the best trade we could have made. One-Three was right; morale would increase because of such a simple addition. They left again, bringing back yet another request for training. However, this time Robin would be joining Two-Five on the training; they had found the group of women that Clay had told us about. We agreed to train them for nothing in return, as they had nothing they could afford to give. The footprint for this one would be small. Two-Five would join the "Trade Team," and they would all remain out for Two days, no more. We decided to suspend our search for others to trade with until they returned, with the Humvee and 240 on call if they needed it.

People I had not seen since the weather turned to shit were out walking around every day; half of them just simply came to say hello. I think I happened to be on their route for long walks. My wife, kids, and I went for a long walk almost daily when I was not working. The team continued looking for other groups to trade with until we were out of things we could live without. Ten groups in all, we took each group radios when we had finished our trading. This gave them the ability to not only call for help but added more lookouts for us further away from our location.

Two weeks had passed when we received a radio call from Clay asking to meet at our "mutual friend's house." Our mutual friend was a guy named Matt. He grew up on a farm two roads over from our location. He moved to Virginia years after high school and later became one of the most successful firearms instructors in the industry. I met him through another friend, and oddly meeting him was how I became friends with Clay. It was a place that only Clay and I were familiar with.

I grabbed my gear radioing to One-three and Six-Six to get ready to go for a walk. We left within an hour, making the three-mile journey to the farmhouse we called V1. The walk was uneventful, which by no means was a complaint, the more uneventful, the better in my book. Once we arrived, we set up overwatch and waited for Clay to arrive. After waiting a couple of hours, I called out over the radio, looking for him.

"Clay, this is Six-Eight what is your current location? How copy," I said.

I attempted this several times, with noting coming back to us. We gave it another two hours before we decided it was best to head back to Main. Something was off, I could feel it in my gut, and I was not alone. Six-Six and One-Three had the same feeling. One-Three radioed back to Main and Two-Eight, asking if all was sunny. Everyone confirmed that our location was still sunny and clear. We quickly packed up and began moving home. We were one mile into our walk back when we got an emergency call from one of the last groups we traded with. With us being away from Main, we decided it best for the truck team to remain at Charlie, and we would check things out.

The closer we got, the more the familiar smell of death became prevalent in the air. We got to within eight hundred yards when One-Three setup the bolt gun. Through the glass, he could see that everyone was already dead. I told him to stay on overwatch while Six-Six and I went for a closer look. We got there, we found one person who was alive but dying, and there was nothing we could possibly do to save him. We moved him into what was left of the structure they lived in, putting him on a table, holding his hand as life slowly left his body.

"Who did this to you?" I asked.

"They had the safe flag," he gasped.

"Who had the safe flag?" I asked.

Before he could answer, he took his last breath, his eyes glazed over as his soul left his body. I swept my hand over his face closing his eyes. Hopefully, his soul will find peace, now that he has left the madness. As we walked around the area, something stood out to me, the radio we gave them was nowhere to be found. We made our way back to the overwatch position.

"Who the fuck called us?" I asked.

"The voice on the other end gave us this location," said One-Three.

"I know, but no one there was alive enough to have called us, it didn't take us long to reach them, and neither Six-Six nor I could find the radio we gave them," I said.

"Something is fucking wrong," he said.

"We should get back to Main fast," said Six-Six.

One-Three packed the rifle up, and we double-timed it back home. Upon our arrival, not a thing at all was out of place, but that feeling hadn't left any of us. We each briefed our individual teams, and then I walked back to Main. I walked through the door to find my wife and Ann sitting drinking tea talking away, unfortunately about me. I asked if the kids were ok and if anything was out of the ordinary around Main, they both replied no, and both asked me what was wrong. I told them that I would be at Alpha for the next few days until the feeling we had worn off.

I called for all team leaders to meet me at Alpha as soon as I got back. I suggested that all team members remain on shift at all times, with no more than two team guys getting sleep at a time for no more than four hours until the uneasy feeling went away. The team voted, and it was approved. Later that day, Richard made his way up to Alpha, looking for me.

"I want to be on the fire team," he said.

"What the fuck brought this up?" I asked.

"I was talking to your wives," he said chuckling, "They told me you have a bad feeling about something, they have no clue what that something is. Then I saw Robin grabbing all of her shit so she could be here full time. My wife saw it too and tried to talk to her about it, and she wouldn't tell her what's going on. I haven't seen any of you guys acting like this since we got here, my family is here, I need to do more to keep them safe. I trained with you before this shit started, I've trained along-side you guys since this shit happened, I'm going to do this and fuck you if you think I won't," he said.

"I wasn't going to say no but understand that any briefings you receive are to remain between us. Some information is kept from the group to keep them from worrying, to help keep them on task and keep panic from setting in. You can't even tell your wife. Understand that if things go wrong on this end, it can cost you your life or the lives of others. You'll be responsible for my life and the lives of those here and at Main. Your family needs to be your last consideration. The lives of everyone else needs to be the focus, with that your family will be safe. If your focus is only on your family, you will jeopardize the lives of everyone here, do you understand me?" I asked

"Yes, I do," he said.

"Ok," I said.

"Can I get a callsign, like you guys have? I think it is cool," he chuckled.

"You are such an ass. What would you like your callsign to be?" I asked.

"Eight-Nine," he said.

I grabbed the push to talk on my radio "Attention team; I would like to formally welcome Eight-Nine to the team, he will be stationed at Alpha, anyone wish to come up see the ass-hat and possibly kick him in the balls, please feel free to talk to your team leaders to schedule that" I said.

Eight-Nine laughed as he walked over to Robin to get everything he would need, that we could spare, to be stationed with us for the duration of the war. The day was coming to an end when we received yet another distress call from one of the groups we had traded with.

This time, it was the group of all women. I called for Six-Six to bring the Humvee up to Alpha to pick up One-Three, Robin and I. Robin needed to go with us because the women there trusted her, and they were more likely to talk to her than if just us guys rolled up. We loaded into the truck and hauled ass to get to them, hoping we would be there in time to help; once on-site, Robin would be in charge.

We turned down the last road to their hide, and we could see the glowing of a massive fire, our fears of being too late came to life the second we pulled up. Robin got out, instructing us to look for survivors, we found no such person. All the women were found stripped of their clothing, hands bound behind their backs, some were tied bent over objects, some were found hanging by their necks. The building they used for shelter was entirely on fire. Robin walked to the tree line looking for a young girl she had seen in her time there. She was only twelve years old. Robin had hoped she fled to the tree line for safety; she found her, but not the way she had hoped for. As she carried the stripped and bound child from the woods, she was crying so hard she could hardly see, let alone walk. One-Three tried to help her carry the child but was told to stay away from her. This loss, I feared, would bring Robin to the point of no return.

Robin insisted on burring the child but refused our help. We all stood watch over her. We freed the bodies of the dead from their restraints, laying them all together and covering their bodies.

"Is that backhoe at the farm, useable?" asked Robin.

"I do believe so. If it is not, I will have my brother start working on it immediately," I said.

"Can we" Robin started to say before I interrupted her.

"Yes, we will, I promise," I said.

The ride back was tranquil; everyone had tears in their eyes. I told Six-Six to park at the farm. We could walk back to Alpha from there. The plan was to gear up for an extended stay while the bodies were buried. I asked Two-Eight to find my brother and tell him to come to see me. When he got over to me, I asked how he had been. We had not talked since Grandpa's funeral. Once we finished the small talk, we discussed the backhoe, last he knew it had been working, I told him to make sure it ran, service it, and get it ready to move. He assured me he would at first light.

I turned to head back up to Alpha when I heard Clay come over the radio for the first time since he blew off our meeting, asking us to meet him at V1 again. I called for Two-Five to get the bolt gun ready to move. We would try this meeting again; however, we were going to go strong. Six-Six got the truck ready again while I called for Ryan, Six-One, and Three-Three to join us at this meeting. We parked a half-mile away from V1 on a side road, making the rest of the trip on foot with Two-Five taking up an overwatch position. He radioed to us everything he saw, for that matter, everything he didn't see. There was no movement, no group of people, there was nothing. The closer we got, the more the hair stood up on the back of my neck. I saw a light coming from inside the barn. We checked for wires around the door and under it as far as we could see. We believed we were clear enough to breach.

In the barn, we found Clay; he had been tortured to death. Once again, he was dead long before he sent that call. He had a piece of paper stuck to his chest. It was a letter to us.

"Dear, Losers whoever the fuck you are, I am coming to your location tomorrow, you have something of mine, and I want it back. I will arrive from the North. I will be traveling with two of my men; we will be unarmed. I wish to discuss the terms of getting what you took back. Even during such times, we can be civilized and discuss things like gentlemen. See you at noon."

CHAPTER 18

"We need to get back to Alpha NOW," I shouted as I turned and rushed for the door. I radioed Two-Five telling him to pack up the rifle and pick our asses up immediately. We didn't wait for him; we started moving towards him until he came along in the truck. We jumped in and floored it getting back as quickly as possible. We gave a quick brief as soon as we returned, then I went back to Main. I wanted to be with my family while I tried to get some rest. I was going to need it so I would not miss anything this guy had to say; every detail could have much larger meanings. It took me some time to fall asleep, trying my best to anticipate what was going to happen, and my biggest question was, what did we take from them, and who are they?

I woke in a panic, and my wife woke to my panic as well.

"What's wrong?" she asked, putting her hand on my arm.

"Just a bad dream is all, go back to bed," I told her.

It took me a while, but I finally fell back to sleep. My morning began like every other; the difference was our enemy had made an appointment with us. I made my coffee, as I sat sipping it, I cut and lit a cigar. I could not tell you what cigar it was if I tried, my mind was to focused on the clock and that god damn dream. Ann walked in as my wife came down the stairs. They talked in the kitchen for a few minutes before walking in and sitting down at the table together.

"Tell me about your dream," said my wife.

"I am fine, just leave it alone," I said.

"I remember when you had bad dreams when we were together, they would affect you all day. Please tell us," said Ann.

"Fuck, seriously, moments like these make me wish you two were still not getting along," I said with a deep sigh.

"Tell us," my wife pleaded.

"All I can remember is getting into a gunfight with the Nazis, they used a 50 Cal, shooting towards the house. When the fight was over, I ran to the house. When I got inside, all I could hear was screaming from the upstairs, and when I got up there, Ann was standing outside Princess' room. As I opened the door, the room was ripped apart, and our kids had been killed by the 50," I said.

"Holy shit," said my wife.

"Do you feel better knowing now?" I asked as I walked out of the room.

I couldn't deal with them at this point, so I walked up to Alpha. Team guys came at me all morning asking questions, everyday bullshit that had been going on, like my cigar, I couldn't tell you what anyone said, I looked down at my watch, it was noon, the day had flown by before I knew it.

"There is a black SUV headed up the road from our position," said Two-Eight over the radio.

I told Two-Five and One-Three to be ready on the bolt guns. Robin and Eight-Nine said they were going to walk down with me, to provide some security for me while I met whoever was in the SUV. I assured them that Charlie team could handle it. Eight-Nine assured me that he would rather be there to be sure. I stripped off my gear, tucking my pistol under my shirt like I used to carry concealed, and we started walking down. The closer we got, I could see the SUV had stopped. Charlie team was confirming that the occupants were indeed unarmed. Two men pulled a table from the back of the SUV and a couple of chairs, setting them up in the middle of the road.

They were no Nazis. They were black, the two who had retrieved the table and chairs had red X's on their jackets. The third man stood six foot five or so. He had on a suit; honestly, it was a nice suit, the kind I always wanted. He looked more like a businessman than the head of a lethal gang. He sat at the table, putting a box on the table as I got closer. Ryan walked up to me before I could sit down. He grabbed my arm and whispered into my ear.

"I know that guy, Robbie, and I used to work with him at the factory, his name is Jimmy."

I looked at Ryan and nodded, then Two-Eight told him and Robbie to check the pasture fence line to make sure we were, in fact alone, he told them to radio if there was trouble. The nice dressed man stood up, holding out his hand.

"I'm King James," he said.

"You can call me Six," I said.

"Ok Six, I was informed that you are a bit of a cigar connoisseur, so I brought a box from my private collection as a gift, to show that we are currently here in peace," he said

"Where did you get your information?" I asked.

"From one of your recently departed friend's group, apparently they do not like being hunted down and killed like the dogs they were," he said.

"I see what do you want?" I asked.

"I know you were present the day the hotel burned to the ground, I know it was you and your men that started the fight that led to my brother's death, it was a smart move turning an alliance on itself."

"I have no clue what you're talking about," I said.

"Don't treat me like I am some stupid fucking animal. I got where I'm at in this life by being smarter than everyone else." he barked.

"If my team was present, what difference would it make? If we were there, I may or may not have seen your brother. If I had, I can assure you he was in perfect health when we parked the truck watching the fight we may or may not have caused," I said.

"The difference it makes is that I want my drugs back, that you and your men stole from me," he said.

"We didn't take your drugs," I said, opening the box of Perdomo Factory Tour Blend cigars he brought, cutting and lighting one.

"His people told me that you and him," he started to say.

"Clay, his name was Clay," I interrupted.

"Ok, Clay's people told me that they saw you and Clay taking stuff from the hotel," he said, lighting a cigar himself.

"We took some ammo, a few guns, and a bottle or two from the bar. We didn't take your drugs. We were back on top of the hill watching to make sure none of the Nazi shitbags made it out of your fight alive when Clay came running from the hotel after he set it on fire," I said.

"You're so willing to give me information, I find that to be a bit cowardice," he said.

I laughed as I exhaled the smoke from my cigar. "You already killed the man. Clay was doing good all-around this town. While my people and I stayed minding our business, what is the harm in telling you the truth? You come here acting like we are all civilized men during this war. We are far less than civilized now. We are all savages, savages trying to survive in this shit. We have no use for drugs here, why the fuck would we take them?" I explained.

"I suppose you're right, but just because we're savages does not mean we cannot act like civilized men. I'll be returning to Goldbeach. I'll have another embassy, you could call it, at the prison, if I happen to find out that you're lying to me, I'll send the full weight of my organization down on you and your so-called team," he said as he stood up from the table.

"I look forward to never seeing you or your men again. I believe that to be in your best interest," I said, holding out my hand. We shook hands, his men packed the table and chairs back into the SUV, and they drove off. I looked at Two-Eight.

"Did the boys report anything?" I asked.

"We haven't heard anything at this time, but you guys have a long fence line. If I hear anything, I will call," he said.

As we walked back to Alpha, I asked Robin and Eight-Nine their thoughts; they both had a bad feeling about the meeting, as did I. Things seemed to be normal for only the next few hours, then we found out what that bad feeling was.

"Six-Eight I need you at Charlie position NOW," called Two-Eight over the radio.

I grabbed my gear and started running down to Charlie, Robin and Eight-Nine were on my six. Everything that could possibly be wrong went through my mind, but nothing could prepare me for the news received upon my arrival. Two-Eight ran to meet me.

"They're gone," he said.

"What the fuck are you talking about? They're gone?" I asked.

"Ryan and Robbie are gone, when they didn't come back, I sent some guys to look for them. I know there has been a lot of tension between them, so I figured they were just fighting in the woods. Six-Six found their radios and guns in the woods on our side of the fence and boot tracks on the other side," he said in a panic.

"Fuck, the fucker recognized them, he must have had guys in the woods on overwatch, and they grabbed them when they got close," I said. My breathing started to pick up; I could feel the world imploding on me.

"I thought they were here in peace?" asked Eight-Nine.

"I remember a quote I had read once. It went something like Civilized men are more discourteous than savages because they know they can be impolite without having their skulls split, as a general thing, the fucker was telling me he was up to no good, and I didn't see it coming" I said.

"What do we do now?" asked Two-Eight.

"We send out a search team, and we find our boys, we bring them the fuck home," I said.

I radioed to Two-Five telling him to have his ass at Alpha by the time I got back. I filled him and the rest of the team in on what was happening when I got there. I started packing my bag. I was planning to be gone as long as it took. When I walked out ready to leave, I was met by Robin, Two-Five, Eight-Nine, and One-Three. Apparently, I was not going to be looking for them alone. We had no clue where to start looking when Robin suggested we start with a recon of the prison since that is where the X boys were holding up.

It would be the early hours of the morning before we got there. It didn't matter at this point. We were going in the same way Two-Five, and I had made our escape from previously; it was the shortest way. After a few hours, we took a short rest, no one said much, the feeling of determination filled the air, and anger weighed heavy in our hearts, heavy enough that the obvious was not realized until we were close to the prison.

"He sure had a hard-on for Clay and his people, didn't he?" I said, looking at the team.

"Yeah, I noticed that too, figured it had to do with the fact that they'd been helping smaller groups of people to be able to fight back," said Robin.

"That would make sense, but there was always an angry tone when referencing them, like when I told him Clay's name, it rolled off his tongue after like he knew it already but refused to say it," I said.

"I noticed that too," said Eight-Nine.

"FUCK ME," I yelled, "They took them to V1. I'll bet anything."

We turned around, making our way back. Hopefully, we would make it in time; God only knows why the hell they were taken. We were moving twice as fast as we started, yet it felt like we were going nowhere. At one point, I found my upper body going faster than my feet, and I ended up tripping over my own feet, going right to the ground. Eight-Nine helped me up off the ground, Two-Five alerted us that we were within a half-mile of V1. He set up overwatch, and the rest of us began our descent to the barn where we had found Clay.

The black SUV from the day took off just as we arrived on the scene. I only saw the two guys in the front that were with the King doesn't mean he wasn't in the back, out of sight. We breached the door, tied to a chair inside the door, was Ryan, he had been beaten to death, tortured, he had a piece of paper stuck to his chest with a knife holding it in place, the note said *LIAR*. His body was still warm, and blood was still dripping off him. We saw that Robbie was tied to a chair as well. He was sitting behind Ryan some thirty feet away, in perfect health.

We finished clearing the area, then called for transport to get Robbie and Ryan's body home. I removed Robbie's gag; he started muttering instantly, still crying after witnessing the tortured death of his brother-in-law. Eight-Nine was untying Ryan as Robbie continued to pace, talking to himself.

"Robbie, you need to get your shit together," I yelled at him.

"They made me watch," he cried out "They made me watch as they tortured him, they went at him for hours before he died."

"I get it. We will get them back for this; I promise you that," I told him.

Robbie punched the wall sobbing, "They fucking made me watch, told me when they were done with him, they would do the same to me if I didn't tell them the truth."

"What the fuck do you mean? Unless you told them the truth? The truth about what," I asked.

"Will they made me watch" he sobbed.

I slammed him into the wall; his shirt clutched in my hands. "WHAT FUCKING TRUTH?" I screamed.

"The drugs Will, the fucking drugs," he screamed.

"Robbie, what the fuck did you do?" The look on my face instantly went from enraged to terrified.

"I told them about the drugs if I didn't, they were going to do the same to me, I saw you and the others offloading them, why didn't you just tell them that you had them?" he cried.

"FUCK" I screamed as I let go of his shirt. I started to walk away when I turned back to him. "Robbie, we didn't take any drugs. We took ammo and cash, that's all," I said.

"What the fuck would we need cash for? I'm not stupid. I saw the trunks; money is useless, so they must have had drugs in them," he said.

"The money is for when this war is over, you asshole, it was going to be divided up between team guys and their families to help us rebuild," I said.

"What?" he looked at me blankly.

"What use would we have for drugs? The money will help us in the end even if it's not worth much; some is better than none," I said.

"I'm sorry, Will, I am so fucking sorry," he began crying again.

"The only reason your ass was at our location was because I found you and your family on my way home, the only god damn reason I took any of you back with me was because of your sister and nephew, now you tell our newest enemy that we have their drugs? You may as well go back and put a bullet in every member of your family's heads," I yelled.

"THEY MADE ME WATCH," he screamed, "what was I sup-posed to do?"

"The team above all else, the team is who protects that worthless ass wife of yours, not you" I drew my pistol, pulling the slide slightly, confirming there was a round in the chamber.

"Will please, you can't kill me," he cried out.

The truck pulled up; the rest of the team turned towards us to see what I was going to do. I stood there for what seemed to be hours, but in reality, it was only moments before dropping the magazine from the pistol; I threw it on the chair Robbie had been tied to.

"I had better not see you anywhere near our location ever again. I have to go back, tell your parents how you let your brother-in-law die, or I can tell them we never found your body, either way, your sister will know the truth. I never could lie to her. There is one bullet in that gun do with it what you will," I said as I turned my back walking for the door.

"WILL PLEASE," he screamed as I walked out.

We loaded Ryan into the back of the truck, we climbed in, as Six-Six put the truck in gear to drive off when we were all startled by the sound of a single gunshot.

We arrived back at Alpha. I sent Three-Three to get Ann, a cigar and a bottle of bourbon. I grabbed another pistol from my foot-locker at Alpha and a holster for it. It was going to be a long night. I cut and lit my cigar while pouring a drink for Ann and myself. She walked up to Alpha, saw me sitting there as I held up her glass.

"Wow, I guess you forgot what happened the last time we had a drink together," she said with a very naughty smile on her face.

"It's not that kind of drink, love," I said, exhaling my cigar.

CHAPTER 19

I stayed up with Ann all night, talking about her past with Ryan and even ours. When she finally quit crying, she staggered over and slept in my hammock. I left it up to her how she explained to her family that her brother was not around. I walked my way back to Main, found my wife, and told her what had happened. I told her where she could find Ann if needed.

"What are you going to do now?" she asked.

"I know what I would like to do, but it is going to have to be a team vote," I said as I poured a coffee.

"What do you want to do?" she asked.

"Kill them all, everyone, that had anything to do with this," I said as I headed towards the cave.

I went downstairs, grabbing myself a cigar, I sat down, my mind was going one hundred miles an hour, I wanted to cry, I wanted to punch something, I wanted to scream, and I wanted to burn the world down all in the same emotion. I waited until I had finished my cigar before radioing the team, telling all team leaders to meet at Alpha in one hour. I made my way to Alpha. I radioed to Two-Eight, telling him to find Carl and send him to Alpha immediately. When the team guys started to show up, I told them I needed to talk to Carl, and then I would deal with them.

"What do you need now?" Carl asked as he walked up, still with his ghetto bebop walk.

"Well, fuck you too very much," I said.

"You only ever want to talk to me when you need me to do something, so what do you want now," he said.

"We need another casket built, and another pallet fire prepped but not started," I said.

"Fuck, who did we lose?" he asked.

"Everyone will be told when the time comes, until then please just get it built and get everything ready," I said as I walked into Alpha to meet with the team.

Everyone who was not part of the rescue mission was briefed on what we found and what that coward Robbie had done. There was a heavy silence among the group. I looked up to see Ann standing in the back.

"We need to retaliate, but the only way that we will is with a team vote. It must be unanimous. Everyone votes, yes, or we do nothing. There is a total of six team leaders for the three teams, plus Eight-Nine and Robin, how do you all vote?" I asked.

Ann spoke up from the back. "I vote yes," she said. "He was my husband, maybe you liked him, maybe you didn't, regardless he was one of you, so I will vote yes for him" she turned around and walked away.

The entire team was for retaliation, but we all agreed there needed to be a solid plan in place. We took most of the day to come up with a legitimate plan, and we began to stage our gear for movement. The eight of us agreed that it would be best to wait until dark before we headed that way. Each team leader selected a trainee who would be in charge until he returned if he returned. We loaded the truck, minus the 240, it was going to remain at Alpha in case they needed it. Two-Five oversaw the first team; he took Six-One, Two-Eight, and Six-Six; I oversaw the second team. Our primary objective was overwatch. I took Robin, One-Three, and Eight-Nine. Six-Six drove the first four-man team down, dropping them off one-half mile from the prison, then he came back for the last three of us. Two-Five, with his team, made their way to the backside wall of the prison.

I took my team to the same burnt up house Two-Five, and I had run surveillance on the Nazis from. From there, we could see that not much had honestly changed since we had been there last. Same military issue Humvees with mounted guns, the same gas tanker trucks, even the same separate space for munitions hell, the only real difference was the color of the pile of bodies in the front lot. Once it appeared to be lights out, I had the idea to see what we could steal out of the munitions tent, they left it unguarded, but from where we were set up, I would be seen on my way to it.

"Two-Five you up to a thieving mission?" I asked over the radio.

"What do you have in mind?" he radioed back.

"We sure could use some special edition boom-boom," I said.

"Copy that," he said, laughing.

Watching through the scope, I saw him come over the back wall, then he disappeared. I noticed him running crates from the back of the tent over to one of the armed Humvees, he must have run thirty crates or more, then a few minutes later, I saw him hauling ass away from the tent, like someone had seen him, but I saw no one chasing him.

"When the fuckers come out the front door, start shooting them," he said over the radio just before the munitions tent exploded.

Robin and One-Three were both on the bolt guns. As the X boys ran out to see what had happened, they started shooting. She shot first, and then him. This kept rounds going down range even when reloading the rifles. Two-Five opened fire on anyone coming from the side entrance as his team all came over the wall, then he threw a frag into the doorway to help seal it off. Eight-Nine and I left Robin and One-Three to run overwatch while we made our way to the opposite side of the prison from Two-Five's team to deal with any of them trying to get outside and flank Two-Five. We shot guys who showed their faces and weapons in any windows we could see. Six-One ran around the back, linking up with us, giving us some frags that had been taken from the tent.

We wanted to avoid going inside the prison. We kept the fight outside so we could not be trapped in a corner. The plan seemed to be working; however, for every one we killed, it seemed two more took their place. Six-Six mounted one of the Humvees and opened fire with a 240 lighting up the entire side of the building. Two-Five threw in a few more frags. It seemed the fight on that side was now over, but on the side we were on, it was far from it. I could see some of the X boys exiting the prison through the yard on the backside. They were not looking for a fight; they were trying to get away. Eight-Nine and I threw frags at the entrance to help close it off, killing a few in the process, but some still got away. Moments later, Six-Six rolled up in another Humvee. This one had a 50 Cal on it; he shredded the side of the building. If anyone was still in there, they were having a bad day as the walls fell in on themselves. We decided to start moving out towards the front when I saw Six-One fall backward. Then I saw a weapon from the window above, I gave suppressive fire from below, when from his back Six-One fired up into the window, first the weapon then the body fell to the ground. It seemed never-ending when suddenly One-Three came over the radio.

"There is a small group of men exiting the front entrance, they have their hands in the air, the fuckers are giving up anyone copy?" he said.

"Good copy," I radioed back as we continued to make our way to the front entrance. Throwing one last frag into the corner entrance to make sure no one came out that way.

"Two-Five is down; I say again Two-Five is down," Six-Six yelled over the radio.

"If he's dead, tell him to get the fuck over it, the fuckers are surrendering," I radioed back.

189

"He took impact to his hard plates, knocked the wind out of him, he'll live, but he's going to be a miserable mother fucker for the foreseeable future," Radioed Two-Eight.

The team made their way to the front as more men walked out, throwing down their weapons, including the two men who had shown up with the King and took Ryan. I stood in front of them, staring at them, on their knees, hands behind their heads, they were saying something, but I couldn't hear anything over my heartbeat.

"Get the SUV, drive it over here, park it, facing the front entrance," I yelled.

Six-Six drove it over, leaving the engine running, I told the King's bodyguards to get in, they did. I began taping their ankles and hands together, and then I taped their heads to the seatbacks. I stepped back from the driver door shooting the one closest to me in both of his knees, then I walked around to the passenger side and did the same; they screamed in agony. I told Six-Six to go and see if there was any fuel left in the tankers; he came back telling me one was near half full. I told him to drive it over to the entrance. We used the hoses on the truck to empty the tanker inside the prison and the SUV as the others who gave up watched.

"What are you going to do to us?" one of them screamed before I tapped their mouths shut.

I put a block on the gas pedal, putting one foot on the brake, I put the truck in gear. "We don't take prisoners," I said, tossing a frag on the passenger seat floor and taking my foot off the brake. The SUV smashed into the side of the prison; seconds later, it exploded.

No one will ever use this facility as a base to hurt others ever again.

The team opened fire on the other X boys. We had no interest in taking prisoners.

We gathered up weapons from the dead and loaded them in seven more Humvees with weapons mounted on them. We drove off, headed back towards center when we were met by a mob of people, men, women, and children all standing there. I was in the lead truck and came to a stop. I got out, a man in the group asked who we were. I assured him that we were not there to do any harm to anyone and that the bad guys were dead until the new ones came to town that was. The truth was they would continue to come, this war was nearly a year old, but it was far from over.

I got back in the truck, and we made our way home. Two-Five was not the only one injured on this mission, Six-Six had been shot in the arm, and Eight-Nine took one in the hard plate as well. We called for Doc to come to check them out and give them their duty restrictions; Doc informed me that Ann had scheduled Ryan's funeral services for the morning. I sat at Alpha for the night. I had a lot of trouble sleeping, as I am sure the rest of the team did too.

Three-Three woke me with a cup of coffee and a cigar. Unfortunately, I didn't have time for the cigar. I needed to be at the funeral, as did all team leaders. I drank my coffee as I cleaned myself up and got dressed. My wife met me at Alpha with the kids, Princess running into my arms "carry me, dada," she pleaded, which of course I did. We got to the funeral location early, my children, as well as Eight-Nine's, picked what flowers they could find for the service.

Ann's parents came to me when they arrived. They were thankful that we had found Ryan and hoped someday we would find Robbie too. I guess I know which story Ann chose to tell them. It was nice that even during such times, she could put aside the differences she had with her brother and give her parents a reason to keep the faith. Midge prepared a lovely service, much like he had for my Grandpa.

We are gathered here today to send forth home to our lord, a warrior, a warrior who fought for us. He fought to keep harm from our doorstep and to keep harm from our hearts. He gave his life in the ultimate sacrifice so that we can continue living free during these very dark times. He is loved for his bravery; he is loved for his strength; he is loved for his sacrifice. Heavenly Father, grant him a place by your side so that he may watch over us and continue to keep us safe during uncertain times. Until we meet again, you, our lost warrior, will not be forgotten in our hearts- Amen.

As Midge lit the pallets beneath the casket, Ann turned and approached me. She asked if we had done what we had promised to do, I assured her we did, I never could break a promise to her. She hugged me and thanked the children for the flowers. Robert stood crying as the fire got bigger. I walked over, standing with him, putting my arm around him.

"I want them dead, William, please can you avenge my dad?" he asked.

"It's already done, kid," I told him, pulling him tighter into me.

"I want to fight, like you guys, as my dad did, I want to be part of the team," he said, trying to keep from crying.

"Your job now, kid is to look after your mom, your aunt, and grandparents, you are the man of the family now," I told him.

"I can fight, you know; I know how to shoot, and I have been at those hand-to-hand classes," he said, beginning to cry.

"I will fight for you, as I fight for all of the people here, you keep your family safe while I keep everyone safe," I said as I hugged him. He cried in my arms for the next twenty minutes, and then he left to be with his mom.

As I walked back towards the house, Doc came to me and asked if we could talk alone. I told him we would meet back at the pavilion in thirty minutes. I geared back up, making my way to meet with Doc.

"What did you guys do last night," he asked me as he approached.

"We sought out the fuckers that tortured our guy to death," I said as I lit a cigar.

"Will, anyone, know it was you and your guys?" he asked.

"I certainly fucking hope not, but I'm afraid that we won't be that lucky," I told him.

"What now, what are we going to do, fearless leader?" he asked aggressively.

"Don't start that shit with me again, I told you before I wasn't here to lead shit, just keep people alive," I growled.

"Is this going to be anything like what we have faced before?" he asked.

"No, when they come, there will be more of them than we have ever seen before, and yes, people will die," I said, looking at the ash on my cigar.

"How do you expect to fight them with only your fucking friends who don't know anything," he said.

"My friends who know nothing. Was it my friends who sent twenty people out looking for shit in places they should never have been looking for things? Was it my friends who sent those twenty people out, that never came back? No, that was you!" I shouted.

"I forgot your plan was the only plan we all needed to follow," he barked.

"No, it wasn't but, it was certainly the one that has worked in this group's favor; I'm sure you're basking in all your glory just waiting for the moment you can say I told you so, but that won't happen, not today. I'm going to take your idea and put everyone with a gun on the front line to fight alongside my men to help us win this fight," I told him.

"It's about fucking time you listened to me," he barked.

"Yeah," I said, walking away.

Neither of us was right from the start. Though my idea had merit, so did Doc's. Though his cost lives in the beginning, my idea was certainly costing lives now. I knew the men that escaped from the prison were headed to the King in Goldbeach. I knew it would take only two to three days for them to get there. We needed to tell everyone the full story so they could prepare. I wasn't ready to call that meeting, but it needed to be done. The King wasn't going to give us a warning. It was going to be a full-on assault and probably from all directions. I went to Alpha, gathering the team leaders. We discussed what was going to be our next step. Once a plan was drawn up, I left to find Doc. I went over the plan with him before leaving it to him to gather everyone at the pavilion so we could break the news.

Everyone arrived; as they all sat at the various tables, I could see the division between those that liked my plan versus those that had liked Doc's plan in the beginning. First, every event that occurred over the last several months was discussed, even the ones we chose not to tell anyone. This, of course, was met with some resistance. Some of the group didn't agree with being kept in the dark as to decisions the team had made. Some even announced the decision to pack their stuff and leave the area before things got too dangerous. Those that did, left the meeting. There were some, who like the others, didn't like being left in the dark, but they were staying.

"What we are asking from those that are willing to remain, there is still so many of you, so many of you with children here, we need everyone who is willing to take up and fight with us to do so. Anyone who is not willing or is not able to fight with us, your sole purpose will be to keep the children safe from harm if we happen to fall." I addressed the group.

Doc assured the group, telling them that this was, in fact, a joint decision that he approved of the plan the team had written up, and this got the rest of the group on board.

"Today, we must set aside our differences. There is a force that will be coming for us. A force like we have not seen before, for that we have been lucky for these past few months. Our luck has now run out.

We must stand together and show these fuckers that sheer will is all we need to defeat them at a game they are very skilled at. I'm asking that you fight with us as if your family's lives depend on it because I can assure you, they do. Make no mistake about it, this will be the fight of our lives, and for some, it will be the last. Today I ask you to stand and fight," I pleaded.

CHAPTER 20

The meeting adjourned, and everyone started going about their separate ways. I tracked down Carl immediately.

"Get the backhoe running, drive down to the farm, and try to dig up the blacktop to try and make the road impassable, then do the same to the East of Alpha," I said.

"That's not a bad idea, but if they're using military trucks, that may not be enough," he said.

"Any other ideas would be much appreciated," I told him.

"I think we should take some of the 2x4s that we had laid by the barn, drive spikes through them, then use the electric drill with the small generator and some lag bolts, if we have any, to mount them spikes up on the road ahead of the dug up blacktop," he said.

"Good call, find yourself some helpers and make that shit happen fast," I told him as I walked towards Main.

Though I knew he was hurting badly, I wanted to find Two-Five, so he could help me close up a route we should have closed a while ago. Four hundred yards past our last cabin, just down from the

Bravo firing station, was a ravine that separated our property from our neighbors. Over the ravine was a one-hundred-year-old tunnel, built with stone blocks that were somewhere close to two thousand pounds each, it let water flow through and was strong enough to withstand the weight of the trains that used to run down the trails. Two-Five stood and one end of the tunnel and me at the other, we pulled the pins on some frags throwing them in as close to the center as possible. Once the dust settled, we looked to see if we had made even a dent in the tunnel, which we did but not enough. After throwing one more each, the tunnel collapsed in on itself, bringing the roadway with it. Now the only way they would be able to attack from that end would be to climb down then back up the ravine.

I left there to see what, if any, progress Carl was having. He had gotten himself a small crew, using everything they could find around the farm, they had started nailing 2x4s and getting them ready to mount on the road. He was working on our small generator; we had not used it since before the war began. It would start but was having trouble staying running. I stood there with him like a nurse to a doctor. He asked for a tool I handed it to him. Felt almost like the old days working on the farm together; he was good with small motors. He got it running, and I started looking for lags. I found enough to put four in each 2x4, for four 2x4s at each of the two roads we were actively trying to close. Once that was done, he went to work with the backhoe digging up the blacktop.

Doc had people working on batches of improvised explosives, little tricks he learned while in Vietnam, anything thing that could be found that if under pressure would go boom. From there, left-over nails, screws, and washers were used to make shrapnel. He had started a weapons collection point. Everything available, not just guns, were to be put in a pile to be handed out later so that all who could fight would be armed. I started to make my way over to him when I was called to Alpha by Six-One

"What's going on, brother?" I asked as I walked in.

"Word on the wire, people, have seen foreign-looking military planes flying overhead, with men parachuting from them," he said with a look of panic on his face.

"Well, that's a big fucking problem to be having, brief the team tell them to keep their eyes on the sky. We could have more problems coming our way than we want to deal with." I told him then I walked back to Main, I had another idea for the backhoe.

I started to head to Main when Robin approached me.

"Is the backhoe working?" she asked.

"Yes, it is, I'm sorry with everything going on, it slipped my mind. When Carl is done with the roads, I'll send him to you, grab some guys and go burry those women," I told her.

"Thank you, Will," she said.

"One thing, the backhoe isn't big enough to dig very deep holes, at most maybe four feet, it won't do better than that I'm sorry" I explained

"It's ok, something is better than nothing, and they deserve something," she said as she walked away.

I caught up to Doc; I suggested small pits, filled with sharpened sticks, like the Viet Cong were known for using. He loved the idea, adding that we could even make shallow two-foot holes, enough to injure and take the enemy from the fight seriously. I told him about the foreign military plane sightings and that he should brief the group. We stood talking for a few more minutes when Ann walked by. She seemed to be smiling for the first time in a while, but not as I knew her too, it was a lopsided smile of content, which caused a very uneasy feeling in the pit of my stomach.

Carl had finished the roads and graves for the women. He tracked down Doc and I. We told him about digging the pits. The three of us determined they would be best place all around the perimeter, especially on the ravine side. He took his crew and chainsaws into the woods to begin work. We briefed the entire group, warning them to stay seventy-five feet from the perimeter at all times. I noticed Ann was not around for the briefing. I left and began trying to track her down, and then her mother approached me, telling me Robbie's wife was missing. I called for a search party to comb the area when I got word over the radio that there were reports of a large number of trucks with weapons mounted headed in our direction. I told Doc to make sure everyone was ready and made my way to Alpha.

I sent One-Three and Two-Five up the road with three extra shooters to try and neutralize as many of them as possible before they got to close. They set up between the bolted 2x4s and the dug-up road. Then we got another call alerting us that the convoy had split off; it was apparent to us that they were not only going to attack from the East of Alpha but from North of Charlie position as well. I notified Two-Eight immediately, he got Six-Six and another shooter set up in two of our trucks with 240 machineguns. I had Three-Three on a 240 in one of the trucks facing the east. It began to snow again at that moment.

The first of the trucks to our East hit the 2x4s. Causing their tires to go flat instantly, by the time the third truck went over, it ripped up from the road, the first truck hit the ripped up blacktop and thank god it sunk in deep the occupants of the first truck were shot up by our guys in the woods just as the second truck came in behind the first. The second truck was as well shot up. The third truck stopped short of the second. Men jumped out using the other trucks as cover; it didn't help them, though. The problem was the next few trucks without flat tires; they drove around the three that were stopped. I wasn't sure how much damage our guys in the woods caused. I could hear gunfire coming from Charlie position when I radioed to Three-Three to open fire, disabling two of them, causing the rest of the trucks to be blocked in behind them. It didn't take long before both guns went dry. Three-Three instructed his driver to back up when the truck beside him got shot up.

Doc had sent people to both sides of the road. They had been hiding in the woods waiting for their moment. I ran from Alpha headed towards the men that were exiting the trucks, that's when the others in the woods came out firing. I ran to the truck still in the road, using it as cover firing at whatever shitbag I could get my sights on, making my way alongside the truck when I saw the driver and gunner had been killed. I kept firing, reloading, and repeating. I looked through to see Six-One on the other side of the truck. I opened the driver door, pulling the driver from the seat, I climbed in, driving the truck towards the fight, parking it with my door facing the enemy.

Six-One continued to use the front end as cover as I climbed into the back, reengaging with the 240; it went dry. I reloaded and continued firing until it was empty.

I climbed out of the truck, looking back at Alpha, I could see Three-Three firing towards Charlie from within the firing station. Just then, I heard the very distinctive sound of a 50 Cal firing. I turned back to the threat in front of us; I could see our fighters still engaging as I came up behind Six-One, putting my hand on his shoulder, so he knew I was there. I tapped him on the back, showing him a grenade in my hand. He pulled one from a pouch yelling "Frag out" as he threw it, followed by me throwing mine. We both moved closer. Robin and Eight-Nine were both hot on our asses. The four of us formed a line, probably not our best decision, firing as we moved towards the trucks ahead. One of the machineguns on top of their trucks opened fire on our people in the woods. It was short-lived as the four of us concentrated our fire on him. Gunfire from three sides was keeping some of the men from being able to get out of the trucks. We tossed more frags out, some landing under the trucks, some made their way into the trucks via the hole the machine gunners never had a chance to come out of.

Two-Eight came over the radio, screaming for our help. Two-Five then radioed to me, telling me he and the others had this area handled. I turned first to head back with Six-One, Robin, and Eight-Nine on my tail. I Radioed Three-Three to hold his fire as we turned down the road in front of Alpha, making our way down to help Charlie team. We split apart, Eight-Nine and I took the left side of the road tree line, Six-One and Robin took a right. We were fifty yards down the road, and there sat a Humvee with a 50 mounted on top, the driver and gunner were both dead, Eight-Nine and I ran to it. He got in the driver's seat, and I got behind the gun.

We started driving down the road, Six-One and Robin got behind us using it as cover as we moved towards Charlie. Their trucks were doing most of their fighting for them, so I immediately directed the 50 to them, then on whatever body I could see. I was hit by bullet fragments from rounds hitting the armor plates around the gun, as the gun went dry. Eight-Nine and I bailed from the truck just as one of their truck-mounted 50s opened up on us. The truck used the machinegun to plow through our trucks, cutting one near in half and causing the other to explode. He continued straight to Alpha. I shot at the tires as it drove by, almost getting shot by Eight-Nine, who was on the opposite side of the road trying to do the same without realizing where I was; apparently, he still had some stuff to learn.

It was firing into Alpha as it continued forward, nearly eradicating Alpha when suddenly the truck veered off course, the gunner still holding down the trigger as a round past through him, he fell, turning the barrel of the gun towards Main. One-Three took both the driver and gunner on his way to provide overwatch with Two-Five. The rest of our group started their way towards the farm firing. Though most of them were hitting noting, we could see some of the X Boys starting to retreat. Betty was officially out of ammo; I picked up an M16 off a dead X Boy and started charging the remaining fighters. I ran over to our cut in half truck. Six-Six was still in the truck; miraculously, he was still alive. I drug him out of the truck, lifting him onto my shoulders, I ran over to the tree line.

As I dropped him, he woke, but he was out of the fight. I called for Two-Four, telling him where he could find him. I ran back towards the truck, again to use it for cover. On my way, I was hit twice in the hard plates and once in my leg. I crawled my way over to the truck and instantly applied a tourniquet. Two-Eight saw me, and he started to run to me when an explosion knocked him back near fifty feet. He wasn't moving, I couldn't tell from where I was at if he was dead or alive, but he defiantly was out of the fight. I moved so that I could fire from a concealed position when I found myself flying onto my back being dragged; Carl had run over, grabbed the drag handle on my carrier, and started dragging me to safety. I fired at whoever I could on my way to the tree line, where I had left Six-Six. I took some ammo from Six-Six to reload my rifle. I continued to fire, taking shots as I could while trying to keep my rate of fire down so we wouldn't be seen.

The gunfire abruptly ceased, like heavy rain that just all of a sudden quit. Two-Four found us in the woods. He immediately applied a bandage to Six-Six's head, told me without a doubt that he had a bad concussion. He made his way to me, the tourniquet was not as necessary as I thought it was, but I was taught, when in doubt, whip it out. The round had passed through my thigh, barely missing the bone. He gave me a compression bandage and went to check on the other wounded. I radioed out, looking for anyone who could bring Six-Six some water to sip on.

Six-One arrived with a canteen for both of us. I drank some before getting my fat ass off the ground, hobbling out to the road when I fell. I started to pick myself off the ground when I looked to my left. There was not much left of our farms. My sister's house was on fire.

People were busy trying to put it out, and our hay barn was utterly riddled with bullet holes. I could even see where what was left of our cows were escaping. My aunt's house was destroyed the pig barn too. I would be amazed at this point if we had any pigs left. There were bodies everywhere, some theirs and some ours. I looked to my right, still trying to get up. Alpha appeared gone entirely, and I saw a couple of bodies hanging off the front wall of it. Others were still headed down to see if they could help. That's when I saw the Humvee again, with a 50 Cal mounted on it. I remembered it had shot towards the house as the gunner was killed.

I found the strength to get up and started moving towards Main. I fell again, I was in no shape to make the walk back, and the cold air was burning my lungs, but god damn, I was going to get there. Every twenty feet, I was picking myself up off the ground, my breathing was so heavy that I couldn't answer anyone who asked if I needed help, let alone where I was going. Eight-Nine caught up to me. He helped me get to Alpha. I'm guessing that's where he thought I wanted to go. I found a tree branch right near what used to be Alpha, it was big enough to use it as a cane to help me walk, and I continued forward.

I could finally see the house, the end where my Princess' room was, had been ripped apart by the 50. The closer I got, the louder my heartbeats became; I could feel it in the pit of my stomach, my worst fears had come true. I made my way up the driveway, again falling to the ground, I was so close, but I had used so much of my strength getting that far, I could barely get up.

I started to hear this high pitch sound, the closer I got, the louder it became. I realized it was the screams of my wife. I made my way into the house, to the stairs, I fell trying to get up them. I got to the end of the hallway to Princess' room, my wife right behind me, putting my hand on the door to open it.

One-Three came over the radio.

"There is a foreign military plane flying over our heads. It's due west of Main. It's flying fairly low, and there's something, oh fuck, it's dropping paratroopers."